CRAVEN'S WAR
BLOOD AND COURAGE

NICK S. THOMAS

Copyright © 2023 Nick S. Thomas

All rights reserved.

ISBN: 979-8327123076

PROLOGUE

Three times the armies of France invaded Portugal and three times they were repelled over several gruelling years. A fourth was stopped at the border with Spain. Yet for all of the success of the Anglo Portuguese army, the armies of Spain continued to be mauled by the mighty host which Napoleon had sent, and they still control most of Spain. But there are many who still resist in spite of devastating victories for Napoleon's forces. The Anglo Portuguese army waits at the border for its moment to strike into Spain, for they cannot remain on a defensive footing forever. Many feel it will come soon, but a bitter winter has led to several quiet months as the armies await the spring and the inevitable advance.

Captain James Craven's recruiting back in England ultimately showed some success, but most importantly it finally put to bed the deadly feud between his brother, Captain William Hawkshaw, and Major Timmerman. A journey back to England had taught them all a lot about themselves, and they had set sail for Portugal together and with a single purpose, to fight the French, and not each other.

Yet uncertainty remains over the strength and intentions of the French armies in Spain, and Craven now commands many untested troops, from common street thieves to proud militia, and volunteers who thought themselves soldiers without ever having seen an enemy. News of Spanish defeats continue to dominate the news and a clash with the vast French forces is imminent. Every fortified Spanish town and city of significance had either fallen or was under siege by the French. A great advance is coming in the New Year, but neither side knows who will make the first move, as both forces rush to gather their strength to deal the first and greatest blow, and Craven must make haste to ensure his troops are ready, no matter where and when the fight comes.

CHAPTER 1

Moxy shivered as he rubbed his hands together and tried to regain some feeling.

"I don't think I could feel the trigger, let alone pull it," he protested in a high pitched and whimsical tone even for a Welshman. He adjusted a length of cloth he wore around his neck as a scarf and continued to rub his hands together as he looked down at his rifle lying seemingly neglected in the front and snow, although the pan was at least kept out of the moisture. He looked upon the weapon with despair, knowing how cold the steel would feel in his hands when he would next have to lift it.

Paget could only nod in agreement as he shivered just as severely, despite having a beautiful, thickly lined winter coat, far superior to the mix of army greatcoats and those they had captured, purchased, or stolen from the enemy or locals. The snowstorms had let up for a merciful moment, but all around them was frost and dense snow. It had been a bitter winter for them all. The snow clung to their coats so much so, they blended in with the bleak scenery as well as green jackets in the autumn.

"It will be Christmas soon," smiled Hawkshaw, as if that was somehow something to look forward to.

It certainly wasn't for Paget, who upon the reminder of such a familial event took out a letter from his coat. It was crumpled and creased. He had clearly read it several times, and once more descended into the writing on it as he thought back to the last horrifying encounter with his father. He had defended Craven and his friends in the face of his angry father, even when they did not deserve his praise in the moment, and that experience and choice plagued his thoughts. He thought he might get some comfort in the letter, but reading it only lowered his mood further.

Charlie wanted to say something and enquire more of his melancholy but was interrupted when Craven leapt into the natural trench where they waited. He looked remarkably enthusiastic and not suffering from the bitter coldness as the rest of them who were whilst waiting idly, for he was breathing heavily from staying active. Paget quickly tucked the letter back into his coat as if to keep it a secret or perhaps embarrassed that he was not at his post and giving his full attention. He looked up to the Captain who had seen the letter but had no time or care to ask after it. It appeared all his thoughts were focused on one thing.

"What news, Sir?" Paget tried to concentrate on his duties, either to be seen to do so, or to take his mind off of his own woes.

"They are there all right, sitting pretty," he smiled.

"Well, what are we waiting for?" Birback growled as he shivered and rubbed his arms and hands as he tried to regain some feeling.

"It is open ground all the way."

They had no horses. They had been left in the safety of the camp, for the conditions and ground were so treacherous, not that it was much better for the soldiers.

"How much do you want this?" Craven smiled back at him.

Birback looked towards the direction from where the Captain had returned and could see only one thing over a verge in the distance, the black smoke of a wood fire burning. And to his frozen hands it was the most alluring thing he could imagine.

"Whatever we are going to do, let us do it quickly," shivered Moxy.

"You would not wait until nightfall?" Craven asked.

"I'd rather face a regiment of French dragoons than sit here a minute more."

Craven could not help but laugh, but he soon realised the concerns were very real. The cold was starting to set in now that he had been idle for a few moments. He looked out at the barren landscape where they were in the mountains dividing Portugal and Spain. They were so few, and there was no backup in sight. Caffy, Ellis, and Vicenta were with them, too, but it was a most modest force. Vicenta looked to be suffering from the bitter cold worse than any of them, and yet she did everything she could to hide it and made no complaints. Craven counted his numbers, which caused Paget to smile, as if that number could have changed since they departed their winter quarters.

"Eight rifles," he declared.

"Will it be enough, Sir?"

Craven shrugged as if he had no idea.

"There's only one way to find out," he smiled as he scrambled back up to the verge from where he had first appeared.

"It's about damn time!" Birback who was merely eager to get moving and generate some heat.

They were all feeling it. For it had been a harsh winter, and that only exacerbated the anxiety they all suffered from as they waited out the end of the year to see what the new one would bring. Although few imagined they would see any movement soon, not in these bitter conditions.

"Two more months of this?" Moxy groaned.

But Charlie shrugged, for as harsh as the conditions were, they were nothing compared to the retreat to Corunna that was always on her mind on such bitter days. She looked around at the barren land with no sign of food nor refuge. It would be a miserable sight if their encampment was not within easy reach. That is what separated the experience from the fateful retreat that always preyed on her mind. There was no rush. There was no forced march, with seemingly no end in sight, and with a whole French army hot on their heels.

The eight soldiers got to their feet with groans for their cold bones did not want to move as much as the minds that drove them onward. Frost cracked upon their coats, dropping away as if they were statues coming to life. They followed Craven on to another verge and stopped briefly where they could get a good look for themselves at the source of the alluring wisp of wood smoke, which they had jealously observed from afar. The source was a charming remote farmhouse, untouched by the horrors of the war and far from any town or even modest village. Loud conversation echoed out from within, and they could see the movement of several horses within a stable nearby.

"You want to do this?" Moxy asked.

"Why not?"

"I wouldn't say we have lived like kings these past weeks and months, but we are hardly starving."

"Is that enough for you? The bare minimum?"

"It's had to be plenty of times in my life," he admitted.

Craven nodded in agreement because it was a hardship he had experienced many times over.

"Are we to risk our lives over this?" Paget asked.

"It's as good a reason as any."

"I am not so sure about that, Sir," groaned Paget.

"Where is your sense of adventure, Lieutenant?" Craven pressed, stunned by the uncharacteristic lack of enthusiasm by the young man.

Paget shrugged, not willing to offer up any excuses.

"Just open ground between here and there," objected Moxy.

"And not a picket or anyone else in sight," replied Craven.

"Enough bloody talking," complained Birback as he lurched forward and leapt over the verge into plain sight. He made his way forward, the frost on the ground cracking and crunching beneath his feet.

Moxy sighed as they had no choice now but to go forward and support the reckless Scotsman. Paget sighed angrily, but he followed on also, as he would not leave his comrades to face danger alone no matter how much he disapproved of their actions. They advanced in a staggered line, creeping forward as if they were thieves in the night, except it was as clear as day. The discussion and laughter from within the house were getting louder as they approached until when they had covered half of the open ground a door in front of them swung violently open. It creaked loudly on its hinges as a cheerful French officer burst out before them, unbuttoning his breeches as he came forward.

Craven and his small band of soldiers stopped, as if by not moving they might not be noticed. Amazingly the Frenchman went on to do his business, laughing to himself as he began to urinate on the frosted ground before him, and yet as he finished, he looked up to behold the nine British soldiers. Their redcoats were covered, but their purpose was obvious to anyone but a fool, as they approached with weapons in hand and bad intentions. The French officer smiled awkwardly for a moment.

"Easy," whispered Craven as if somehow the situation could be calmed. The Frenchman studied them and could see their British issue equipment and swords, which Craven and Paget had drawn and readied for action.

"Anglais!" He suddenly rushed back to the doorway.

Birback stormed after the man as if to catch him before he could get back to safety. He reached the door just as it was slammed shut with his fingers trapped. He winced as he pulled them free, but they were mangled and bloody.

"Bastard," growled Birback as Craven slammed into the wall beside him, eager to get away from the windows from which muskets and pistols might be fired from. Low and behold a shot soon rang out, and another window was smashed open before a shot rang out from the far side of them.

"Now look at what you have done," moaned Craven to the bloody Birback who stared at his gnarly hand with disgust.

"Me? How could I know the bastard would take a piss?"

"Maybe if you had waited a little longer!" Craven yelled.

"Wait? How long would you have us wait and freeze our bollocks off?" Birback failed to contain his anger.

Craven shrugged, having no answers for him. He tried the heavy door to find it was bolted firmly shut.

"Ah…to hell with it." Birback wailed and stepped back from the wall. He took a short run at one of the windows, crashing through it like a wrecking ball with no finesse at all and drawing cries of panic from the defenders.

"Christ," sobbed Craven at how the plan was so rapidly falling apart. The others all took shelter under the wall of the house and looked unwilling to move, except for Vicenta, who was nowhere to be seen.

"Paget, on me! The rest of you, shoot something!"

Craven led the way forward around the house until they reached the main front door just in time to see Vicenta shooting at the lock with a pistol. She smashed her body into the door, and it blew open. She vanished inside with the sound of cold steel soon echoing out.

"Well how about that, Mr Paget, would you have a woman lead the way?"

Craven was doing his best to rile up the young officer and incite some passion. Paget sighed angrily as he pushed past Craven and rushed on through the doorway. Craven smiled, having at least achieved his goal. He ran on after the two of them with pistol in one hand and sword in the other. He got inside to find Paget had already run one man through. Vicenta had vanished into another room, but he could hear the chaos that she was causing. He rushed on to help Paget and cut down a trooper who rushed towards the young Lieutenant.

The farmhouse was remarkably spacious, but Birback was crashing about like a raging bull as he fought two officers with his bare hands. He had the blade of one of the Frenchmen locked firmly in his left hand whilst he had his other hand on the throat of the other. He soon brought the two men together, causing them to crash into one another before he drove his knee into the face of one and smashed the head of the other into a tabletop. He lost his grip of the sword but reached for a heavy metal pan and parried away a cut, smashing it into his attacker's head before tossing it at the other. Both men fell to the floor unconscious. Birback was breathing heavily, but not as much from exertion but from anger as he had whipped himself up into a rage.

"Leave some for the rest of us," Craven said to him.

"More!" Birback picked up the iron pan from the ground rather than draw his sword, for he was quite partial to the barbaric and primitive concussive force as if he were some ancient men with a primitive club, and that suited him just fine.

"Captain!"

Paget suddenly came to life as he pointed past Craven to an attacker behind him. He turned just in time to see a pistol directed at his chest and cut down at the muzzle with his sword. The powder flashed as the weapon lowered. The shot was still released, and Craven felt the flame of burning powder scorch his leg as it burnt a hole through his coat. Fortunately, the thick fabric had been enough to save him from any serious harm and returned fire, giving his attacker both barrels in return for the cheek of trying to shoot him in the back. His attacker went down, but flames rose up his coat, and he rushed to take it off and stamp out the flames. He smelt thoroughly smoked as though he had been sitting too close to a fire all day with his hair burnt at the ends, but he sighed in relief just as Vicenta appeared before them, having cleared the rest of the ground floor by herself. There was blood on her face, but it didn't appear to be her own, and yet gunfire still rang out from upstairs and outside as the battle continued to rage on.

"Let's end this," growled Craven.

But Vicenta was already ahead of him. She rushed on up the stairs, and he tried to keep up. She ran the first man through before he had even reached the top of the stairs. He found several cavalrymen hurrying to reload their carbines as one fired out of the window without a target, as if hoping to cause enough noise to drive their attackers away. It was as if somehow, they thought they were under attack by a weak-willed group of bandits or even wild animals. Craven smiled, as his friends were a mix of both. The cavalrymen drew swords as he went forward, but there was little space to swing their long heavy sabres. He drew his dirk and merely used his sword to smother theirs as he ran them through at close-range.

Paget was in amongst them soon enough, his short stature being quite the advantage in the modest room as his blade did not strike the ceiling when he lifted it to cut. He darted amongst two of the cavalrymen, fencing off their blows with ease as they had no room to swing with any power. They could hear a war cry ring out and a crash as Birback raced up the stairs, bouncing off the walls like a raging bull. He grabbed one of the men fighting Paget and tossed him out of the window like a rag doll. The man crashed down beside Moxy who looked amused before the man reached for the sword he had dropped. Moxy quickly readied his rifle and shot the man dead before he could get to his feet. The Welshman backed away from the house and watched with amusement as he could see the flash of movement through the broken windows on the upper floor. The firing had stopped now as the melee ensued and soon went quiet. Hawkshaw had not moved from cover the whole time, his pistol and sabre in hand ready for a fight which never came.

"Is it over?"

The bolt of the door which has been slammed onto Birback's fingers swung open, and the rough and rowdy Scotsman appeared before them. His mouth was bloody, but he smiled, baring his bloody teeth proudly, having greatly enjoyed himself.

"Welcome, gentlemen," he smirked.

Hawkshaw released the lock of his pistol to return it to the half cock before stuffing it back into his officer's sash, but he kept his sabre in hand as he entered the house with suspicion.

"There it is, lads," smiled Craven as he came down from the stairs and drew their attention to the large fireplace. It was a lavish affair for the country, where few houses had any at all. At the centre of the pit still cooking was a boar, for which Birback gazed upon with glee as he licked his bloody chops and began to drool.

"Was it worth it?" Hawkshaw asked.

"You jest?" Charlie looked upon it with almost as much jubilation as Birback.

"You think so?" Hawkshaw pressed Craven for a reply.

"A lot of men would kill for such a fine feast."

"Is that not what we have just done?"

"We?" Craven answered, knowing his brother had not

joined in the killing.

"You know to what I refer."

"They are the enemy, and it is my duty to seek them out and kill or undermine the efforts of the enemy at every opportunity, is that not what we are here for?"

"And it just so happens to suit you, too?" Hawkshaw replied to him accusingly.

"Can a man not do his duty and profit from it at the same time? Is that not the dream?"

"Uhhh…. Captain…" declared Paget in a concerned tone.

Craven knew the Lieutenant's worries were never without cause, and so he rushed to join him.

"What is it?"

But Paget need not answer as he could see for himself. More than forty dismounted French cavalrymen were climbing the hill towards them with musket and sword in hand.

"Now you've really stepped us in the shit!" Hawkshaw roared as he got a good look for himself.

The Frenchmen did not wear any winter protections. They must have come from several of the buildings lower in the valley where smoke arose from two more chimneys, which had been disguised from a distance by the main house. They were only a minute or two from reaching the house Craven and the others now occupied.

Birback got a good look for himself and simply burst out into a maniacal laughter. It was as if he relished the opportunity, despite still bleeding from his last encounter with the enemy.

"Ready your weapons. Gather every French pistol and musket you can find and have it ready to shoot!" Craven ordered.

But nobody moved.

"Well? Get to it!"

Paget was amazed it had to be said, and that Hawkshaw was too dazed to repeat the order. Moxy rushed upstairs with Ellis and Caffy as they moved to take up firing positions on the floor above.

Craven began reloading his double-barrelled pistol as he kept an eye on the enemy advance.

"After everything that happened in England, this is what we came back for?" Hawkshaw asked.

"Nobody said you had to come back, but if you are going to stay, then you better start fighting!" Craven picked up a French musket from the floor and thrust it into his brother's hands. He then reached for a cartridge box and threw it at him.

"What am I supposed to do with this?" Hawkshaw asked in disgust.

"Five times our number of Frenchmen are climbing that hill to come and kill us. Either we dissuade them, or otherwise we'll have a hell of a fight on our hands."

"Isn't that what you always wanted?" Hawkshaw asked grumpily.

"To be drowning in Frenchmen? No, I came here to win." Craven smiled back at him.

Hawkshaw protested no further and loaded the enemy weapon with a sullen expression on his face, the sort a common soldier wore when ordered to latrine duty. Craven finally withdrew his ramrod from the second barrel and readied his formidable pistol before taking another glance at the enemy. They could hear the Frenchmen yelling out angrily as if expecting to make them flee with harsh words and a menacing advance. It would be enough to see many a group of outnumbered soldiers off, but Craven looked back at the hog over the fire and licked his chops as he imagined them all digging into the mighty feast.

"It's not too late to run," insisted Hawkshaw.

But Craven shook his head as he took up a French pistol from the floor and went about loading it.

"We didn't endure the frost for all of this day to return empty-handed."

"Returning without a casualty is far from empty-handed."

Craven sighed angrily and took one last glance to be sure of the enemy distance before turning to his brother.

"I know why you would not kill Timmerman, but here against the enemy, you must not hesitate."

"You couldn't kill him either, could you?"

Craven was stunned as he realised it was true. He had imagined himself running his old nemesis through so many times, and yet when he had the chance, he showed mercy.

"Maybe that bitter bastard has a place yet in this war. There is no denying he is a tempest, so long as he can be blown in the right direction," admitted Craven.

Gunfire rang out as several pistols and muskets were fired at the house. One shot smashed through the window between the two officers and struck the wall on the far side of the room. Craven peered out from the broken window whilst Hawkshaw remained firmly out of sight. It was as if he had truly started to value his own life and shrugged off the carelessness of youth he had exhibited so proudly when Craven had first known him. Yet Craven could see it was not the accurate fire of sharpshooters that had struck the window, but the wild and sporadic fire of a mob. They approached without formation or any kind of tactics, as if their mere presence would be enough to scare off Craven and his comrades. Craven smiled.

"What is so funny?" Hawkshaw was horrified.

"They think they are dealing with a few poachers."

"Aren't they?"

"You forget yourself, Captain, and what you are," smirked Craven.

"And what is that?" Hawkshaw sounded uncertain.

"A killer."

That didn't do anything for Hawkshaw's nerves, and the realisation it was an accurate assessment only made him feel more uncomfortable.

It was in this moment that Craven could see Hawkshaw had lost his stomach for war. Perhaps it was the tumultuous affair with Timmerman or the bitter winter they had endured, but he no longer wanted any part of it. Craven's gut reaction was to ridicule him for it, and yet he understood as he thought back to their first encounter. Hawkshaw came to Portugal to settle a matter of honour, not anything more, and yet it reminded him of his own arrival and how different his expectations had been. Craven had been determined to never see a Frenchman throughout the entire war. He smiled at the prospect.

"What is it?" Hawkshaw asked in astonishment at his expression.

"I came to Portugal to find my fortune, and right about now that hog over there is the greatest fortune I can imagine."

Hawkshaw looked at the carcass that was still cooking over the fireplace and seemed to relax a little.

"You didn't just come here to fight and to kill?" he asked

in amazement upon the realisation that Craven really was there for the meal for himself and his comrades.

"I'll fight for many things, and a good meal is high on the list."

Hawkshaw looked about the room at the others to see firm agreement, even from Paget. Seeing Birback's barbarity made him fear he was following a similarly depraved route and that they were all sinking into it. Yet now he could see that Craven's intentions were pure. He lifted his musket up and moved to the window that had just been shot out, determined to do what needed to be done. He had a clear view of the enemy mob advancing towards them with wild cries as some whirled sabres about their heads. Two more shots rang out, striking the walls of the farmhouse.

"We have to make them want no part of this," declared Craven.

Hawkshaw nodded in agreement.

"Give them everything you've got!" Craven shouted as he readied his French pistol and pointed it out at the French and fired. A staggered volley rippled out from the house, causing a thick fog of powder smoke through which they could only just make out some glimmers of movement as the enemy continued to advance.

Craven took up his double-barrelled pistol and fired off his first shot. Hawkshaw let loose also, and Craven then fired again. Another smattering of shots rang out from both floors of the farmhouse, and in the silence which followed he could hear the clang of ramrods from his comrades hurrying to reload; including Hawkshaw who no longer protested and hurried to load the musket as if a regiment of cavalry descended upon him.

The French returned fire as cries still rang out as they made their advance. Craven rushed to load the French pistol, knowing he would never reload both barrels of his own prized weapon. He had just pushed the wadding of the cartridge down the muzzle when he caught a glimpse of movement in front. He hurried to cock the pistol and present it towards the enemy as if to shoot, despite knowing it was not ready to fire, for he had not rammed the load home. But fire rang out from those who had loaded more quickly, and even though the guns fell silent, a French officer stopped before him, looking down the barrel of his pistol. He looked exhausted and his moustache and uniform were scorched and blackened by powder smoke and burns.

The man stopped and folded over a little as he coughed his guts out and tried to wipe the soot from his face, even though he knew he was standing in the line of fire. Several more of the enemy troops appeared beside him. Two were wounded and all looked exhausted and demoralised, with no fight left in them at all.

"C'est fini," the officer declared. He nodded towards Craven and the others, accepting defeat but also pleading for no more punishment without actually saying the words.

Craven first looked to Hawkshaw and could see he was on the edge of losing his brother's support. He looked back to the Frenchman and nodded in acceptance, but he could hear the scrape of a ramrod and looked over to see Charlie eagerly reloading.

"That's enough," he ordered.

"Why? Because they say so?"

"No, because I do! Leave them be!"

Charlie looked furious, and yet when she noticed Paget

pleading with her to comply with his puppy-like eyes, she backed down.

"They'll live to fight another day," she groaned.

"Yes, and so will we," replied Hawkshaw with relief.

Craven watched the enemy pick up their dead and wounded as the intoxicating cloud of powder smoke began to dissipate, and he was finally convinced it was over. He turned his back to the wall beside the window from which he had fired and slumped down to the floor with a sigh of relief.

"You know someday this war will be over," declared Hawkshaw.

"Yes, and then I might have to find a real job," smiled Craven.

CHAPTER 2

"What do you call that, Nooth!" Matthys roared as he watched Joze get the better of the former militiaman with a singlestick, the same man who had only a few months ago given Craven a good run for his money, even if the Captain was not in the best of shape at the time. Nooth was bleeding from the cheek where he had been dealt a smarting blow, and yet the fire within him was gone now. He no longer had his competitive streak nor enthusiasm.

Drills continued on in the distance as the enthusiastic sergeants drilled the troops to keep them in shape during their time in winter quarters. They trained in a small field normally used by cattle but had been taken over by the army. It was situated in one of the great many villages across the Portuguese border where they waited for the bitter season to come to an end. It was not the respite many had hoped it would be. For not only was the weather wet, cold, and miserable, but their future remained most uncertain, and rumours of French forces gaining momentum and strength in Spain ran rife. Nooth gave up his contest as he went to Matthys to air his frustrations.

"What is it all for? Months of sitting about here and nothing?"

"Is that not what you did in England?"

"We might as well have stayed there until the war was ready for us," he protested.

"Is this your idea of a soldier? The easy life until it suits you?" Matthys recoiled.

"It's how Captain Craven lives, is it not?"

Matthys shot him a scathing look as he prepared his bitter response.

"Captain Craven has lived through more hardship than you can ever imagine. Whilst you were back in England playing at being a soldier, he has been out here fighting year after year."

"I know, and that is what I came here for, but all we do is sit about doing what we did back home but in worse conditions," admitted Nooth in a mix of frustration and agreement.

"You'll get your chance, and when you do, you may well wish the winter had lasted a few weeks longer."

Nooth smiled as he suspected the Sergeant might be right. He took a breath and calmed himself. He looked out at the drill being conducted by several bodies of redcoats as their sergeants continually barked orders.

"The infantry march and they drill, and yet we fight with sticks? Mathewson was always so eager to do the same, and yet nobody else does it?"

"Even Craven will admit that the sword has so little place

in the infantry anymore, and yet we are not the infantry."

"We are not?"

Matthys shook his head and smiled.

"Then what are we?"

"Quite honestly, I am not sure even Lord Wellington knows, but he can see the results we achieve, and so that is all that matters."

"Riflemen are quite the rage now, aren't they?"

"Yes, but Craven is no rifleman. He can barely even operate one," smiled Matthys.

"If not riflemen, nor infantry, and we are certainly not cavalry, I wonder what our role truly is."

"More like hunters," admitted the Sergeant.

"Caçadores, that is what the Portuguese call men like Captain Ferreira, is it not? Hunters?"

"They do."

Nooth appeared to be deep in thought.

"What is it now?"

"Tell me honestly, Sarge. We all hear the rumours and what is written in the news, but does Craven really fight this war with his sword?"

"The Captain fights with everything at his disposal, and his most powerful weapon are the fighters who stand side-by-side with him, but yes, the regular use the Captain's blade sees would make a heavy cavalry trooper fall silent in bewilderment."

"How in this war of muskets and rifles and grand artillery batteries, how does he achieve so much with a sword?" Nooth asked in amazement.

"There is more to war than thousands of soldiers marching out before one another and expending black powder.

Lord Wellington is more formidable than a thousand men on the battlefield, and yet the only weapon he utilises is his mind."

"You'll forgive me, Sergeant, but as impressive as the feats of Wellington are, the General commands men to fight for him, but Craven does the fighting himself. And that is hardly a fair comparison, is it?"

"No, and yet it remains true. You were an experienced militiaman, and I know what that is like, and so does Craven. Not to disparage your efforts, but the militia and the volunteers play games that mimic war, but they are not war. During those games a volley or a cavalry charge is enough to finish a foe or make them run, but in real war it often takes much more. It is there that cold steel is required, and that is just the battlefield, for Captain Craven's successes are mostly achieved long before two armies ever meet."

"How so?" Nooth asked with much curiosity. The doubt had now faded from his mind, and he genuinely wanted to learn more.

"What happens on a battlefield can change the course of the war, but what if a thousand men on the opposing side never reach that battle? What if that enemy is robbed of hundreds of barrels of gunpowder? What if the enemy is in the wrong place at the wrong time? What if the morale of the enemy can be reduced before they are ever encountered? Captain Craven cannot win battles by himself, but he can make sure to tip the scales in ways most will never see."

"You are talking about the work of spies and agents. Dirty work in the shadows?"

"Sometimes, yes, it is indeed that."

"But is that soldiering?"

"If Craven's sword could talk, you would have your answer." But he said it solemnly, thinking of the death and destruction that the sword had caused in the Captain's hands.

"And I thought I came here to march before the French and give them what for."

"No, you came here to fight for Captain Craven, but you can always leave anytime you want."

"That is not how the Army works," declared Nooth.

"The Army? No. You would be on a charge and be considered a deserter. The provosts would hound you all the way back to England and beyond. But here? You serve only one master, Captain Craven, and he can't afford to have men beside him who do not believe in what we are doing. We are in this until the end, no matter what," replied Matthys pensively.

"And that rests heavily on your heart?"

"Killing is against God's will, and it brings me no joy to take a man's life."

"But you do so?"

"I do what I must, and that is what you must do also. I know you can fight, but it remains to be seen if you can fight the enemy, and fight when your opponent genuinely wishes to take your life."

"I know that I can."

"Then stop this belly aching about the weather and conditions we face here. For they are nothing compared to the hardships you will face before the enemy. Enjoy this time we have here, because come the spring all hell will surely break loose."

"You really think so? You think Wellington will finally ride into Spain once more?" Nooth asked enthusiastically.

"Something has to change. Either we advance, or the French do."

"Then let them come. I most certainly want my chance at 'em."

"Don't be so eager to see the enemy, for they will not be all you imagine them to be."

"How so?" Nooth sounded amazed, almost stunned by Matthys' lack of enthusiasm to do battle.

"This fire you feel in your belly, the French soldiers feel it, too, and they will try just as hard to kill you as you will try against them. Remember that."

"I will welcome it," insisted Nooth.

Matthys shook his head as he knew there would be no changing his mind, and yet it was Nooth who pressed now as he was seemingly disappointed by the Sergeant's lack of fight.

"You've been here for a few years, so how can you not eagerly await your next shot at the French?"

"I came here to win, not to kill."

"How can you do one without the other?" Nooth argued.

"Many battles have been won without the need to spill blood!" Matthys sounded stern as if angered that he needed to justify it.

"You dream. This war will not be won with words, but with the musket, the gun, and the sword."

Matthys smiled and offered no response as though he knew more than he was willing to let on, but no longer had the energy to argue.

"Just don't be so eager to seek battle, for it will find you soon and often enough."

"I truly hope so," groaned Nooth as he went back to his

training.

"The naive enthusiasm of youth," declared Ferreira. He had been sitting on a barrel nearby listening in and providing no insight or help. He wore a very thick greatcoat he had taken from a French officer and held a mug of steaming hot fluid in his hands.

"I suspect you never suffered such an affliction?"

Ferreira laughed as it could not be truer.

"I think I might have once shown to be so bright and foolish when I was but a small boy," he admitted.

"Nooth is anxious and eager. Perhaps they are ready, but many a man such as him is reckless in the face of the enemy."

"And what is Craven?"

"A reckless fool, but one capable of digging himself out of the hole which he dug for himself," admitted Matthys.

"Are you sure about that?" Ferreira was remembering the dangerous battles they had fought in the past to save their roguish commanding officer.

"Well, no, but he's not dead yet, and many a soldier I have heard speak like Nooth is long dead and buried, and they will not be the last," replied Matthys solemnly.

Ferreira shrugged as he tried to not let the losses ruin his mood and drag him down into the ruinous despair he had seen some others fall.

"How about you? Your country is now safe. If we march into Spain, will you come?"

Ferreira seemed to be stunned by the question.

"My country is not safe until the French are driven back into France and crippled so severely that they may never march across Europe ever again," he declared sternly.

"Then you are in this fight until the end?"

"I never thought I would say it, but yes, I am."

Matthys looked impressed, as he could see how far the Portuguese Captain had come, and it reminded him of Craven's own journey. For which he had played such a vital part, and yet he could see the weight of their situation sat heavily Ferreira's shoulders, and he knew why.

"You have heard the news from across Spain?"

"I have."

"The Spanish armies and cities are falling across the country."

"Yes, they are."

"And that does not concern you?" Matthys pressed.

"A little, but we can undo all of that just as soon as we can get back into the fight."

"And if we cannot?"

"It is not like you to doubt. Is God not on our side? Is that not what you think?"

"Yes, always, but we also have free will, and we make our own destiny."

Ferreira groaned as if he didn't care.

"The stakes for the New Year could not be higher. The stalemate cannot last. Either we make great gains in Spain, or we lose all of Portugal."

"Then let it be the former," declared Ferreira.

"And if it is not?"

"Then I will soon be returning to England, and not just for a few weeks."

"You would go? You would flee to England and leave your country to the French?"

"I would go wherever I can keep fighting," declared Ferreira proudly.

"You think this war would continue after the loss of all of Portugal and Spain?"

"Yes, because England is a stubborn place full of stubborn fools."

Matthys shrugged and smiled as he could not doubt it.

"When was the last time your country was successfully invaded?"

"Not since William the Conqueror."

"Yes, and so you see, I will put my faith in the stubborn little island which has been a thorn in the side of the French for as long as both nations have existed."

"It's the Captain!" roared one of the volunteers who had travelled with them from England.

Ferreira leapt to his feet to see Craven and the others striding triumphantly towards them. Caffy and Birback carried the wild boar they had taken, still on the spit, and slung across both their shoulders. Cheers rang out as they approached, and the soldiers of the Salfords salivated at the prospect of fresh meat. The Captain looked most pleased, but Matthys was just glad to see them all return in one piece as cheers rang out. More than anything the troops were glad of a break in routine and something to get excited about after the endless training and miserable winter conditions.

"Get cooking, we will eat well tonight!" Craven called out excitedly, eliciting another cheer.

"Stop right there!" roared an imposing voice as a British officer raced onto the scene, "You are thieves I say!"

Craven looked to the others with amazement and

bewilderment, as he did not recognise the officer nor have any idea as to what he was referring to. Only Matthys looked genuinely concerned, for he would not at all be surprised to find Craven had taken the prize from an ally. The furious British officer stormed up to them and soon targeted Craven as the man in charge, owing to his uniform.

"You, Sir, are a thief!"

Craven smiled and shrugged as it was not untrue, and yet he laughed as he knew his latest prize had been taken from the hands of the enemy.

"The fine animal came directly from French hands, I will have you know," he replied whimsically as if the man would take his word and drop it.

"I do not believe you, Sir!"

"And I don't care."

"You are a liar, Sir!" The furious man shouted back at him.

Craven's humoured expression soon faded away. He turned back to the angry officer and strode up to face off against him with a grim and serious tone.

"And so what is your name?"

"Captain Harding."

"Well, Harding, I suggest you get out of my face and find your own hog, because this one is ours."

"What is the meaning of this?" Major Spring raced onto the scene, much to the relief of Matthys and Paget who watched in horror as the scene descended into what would inevitably be bloodshed. The Major placed himself between the two Captains and ushered for them to give him some space.

"Now, what is the meaning of this?" Spring demanded.

"Sir, as you are aware, only two days previously I reported

to you the theft of two turkeys and one sheep from my possession," growled Harding.

"Indeed, Captain."

"And now today, this vagrant returns to camp with yet another animal for his vagabonds to feast upon. They are thieves, and I am certain of it," Harding raised his voice for all to hear.

"Well?" Spring asked Craven.

"It's true we stole this feast, yes, but not from any British hands, nor our allies. This animal was paid for in gunpowder and blood."

Birback grunted in approval as he was still nursing his smashed fingers. His face was covered in dried blood from the shattered glass that had fallen over his head as he had tumbled into the farmhouse where they had found the animal.

"No thief would travel all the way to French lines to take what he could steal here from under our noses," Harding sneered at Craven.

Spring once again looked to Craven for answers, but he sighed in frustration as he had no way to prove his claim.

"These animals were destined for the officers' mess, and they have been stolen out from under us by men who wear the same uniform."

Craven shrugged as he had nothing to say.

"Captain Harding, you have lost valuable animals intended to provide a good meal, and Captain Craven, you claim innocence whilst being in possession of an animal which would indeed be hard to find in these lands. Will neither of you concede?"

Craven grumbled angrily.

"I will not!" Harding cried.

"Then we must compromise. Captain Craven, you will hand over the carcass to Captain Harding, and we will consider this matter closed," declared Major Spring.

"This bastard loses two turkeys and a sheep, and now he gets our pig as compensation! The same pig we risked our lives for," protested Craven.

"I will see this matter closed," demanded Spring before taking a few steps closer to Craven and leaning in to whisper in his ear.

"Listen, Captain, I know you have been dipping in and taking food and wine from more than a few officers' mess. Let this go, and I will consider past indiscretions a closed matter."

Craven groaned as he finally nodded in approval.

"Good, then the matter is closed!"

Harding signalled for two of his men to reclaim the carcass, but to the chagrin of Craven's comrades who watched as their dinner was taken away. Craven sighed angrily as his hand fidgeted over the hilt of his sheathed sword in frustration that what was rightfully his was being taken away without a fight. Yet he knew there was nothing he could do about it.

"Now, Captain Craven!" Major Spring shouted at him. The group was silent as they awaited their fate, "Now you are through stealing from our own, it is time you stole from the enemy instead!"

Craven shook his head in disbelief.

"Where do you think we got that damned pig?" he complained.

"We aren't fighting over scraps here, Captain, we are fighting a war! Report to me at first light, and you will ensure your men are ready to march, for I have work for you!"

"Yes, Sir," Craven sighed loudly, not bothering to disguise it.

CHAPTER 3

Craven watched the flicker of the fire as he listened to the grumbles of those around him. They had salivated earlier that day at the hope of freshly cooked pork, and now they went hungry on army rations, which were just enough to survive but did not bring them any joy. Few of the houses had fireplaces, and so they spent many a night outside around a campfire before settling down to their cold beds each night.

"I bled for that meal, and now what have we got?" Birback groaned.

"Your freedom, and no lashes," replied Charlie as she knew how harshly the treatment could have been.

"What's mine is mine, and any man who would come and take it should have to fight me for it," he complained.

The rumblings went on between them all, but nothing came of it. Morale was low, and Craven was painfully aware of it, which is why he went looking for such a feast in the first place.

"Did you really take it from the French?" Matthys sat down beside him.

"Does it matter?" Craven scowled back at him.

"It matters to me."

Craven nodded in agreement as he cared far more about what his old friend thought of him than any officer in the army, and even Wellington himself.

"French bastards gave us a hell of a fight for it, but you knew that, didn't you? I am sure you already learnt everything you needed to know from Mr Paget."

"I would have hoped so, but the Lieutenant is rather out of sorts."

"Why?"

"I haven't a clue, but I imagine you would know better than I."

"Why the devil would that be?"

"Because you are the cause of most of the ups and downs in that young man's life."

"Not all of them," smiled Craven as he looked for Charlie, knowing how close she had become with the Lieutenant, but he found her gazing intently. He then followed her gaze to find Paget sitting alone. His right hand was rested inside his jacket as if holding onto something dear and of great value and importance. Craven was instantly reminded of the letter he had seen the young officer stuff into his coat and hide from him just before they attacked the farmhouse. Yet none of this gave him any of the answers he wanted.

In previous years he would have brushed it off and moved on. For the woes of others were rarely his concern, but things were different now. He cared for those around him, and few as much as he had become endeared to as Paget, who had become as a little brother to him of sorts. Craven went to him and found him to be just as defensive as before. He took his hand from his coat and tried to keep whatever was inside a secret. The Captain sat down beside him and took in the warmth of the roaring fire. What was often an annoying and stifling wood smoke was quite the relief in these wet and cold days, where their uniforms and lodgings were perpetually damp to the touch and smell. Wood smoke did a great deal to mask it well into the next day, whilst they would all spend as much time about the fires as they could to dry their clothing and warm their bones.

"Good evening, Sir." Paget tried to act his normal self, but he could not hide his sadness, which muted his tone and took the shine from his youthful enthusiasm.

Craven sighed as he knew he was going to have to press the young man in a way he was not at all experienced, for he was far better at letting his sword do the talking.

"What is it, Sir?"

"Most of the men are down this night because we lost our prize and a damned fine meal."

"Yes, Sir," Paget agreed.

"But you are also down, and it is not for the same reason, is it?"

Paget looked away and stared into the fire as he ignored the question.

"That letter in your pocket, did it bring bad news?"

Paget sighed as he thought he had kept it a secret, and yet he still kept his eyes locked on the fire before finally replying.

"The letter is from my father."

Craven nodded in agreement as he now understood to

some degree why Paget was so distracted. He only had a vague memory of the man from their lone meeting. He had been in a drunken state, but the memory was vivid enough to remember the heated tension on that occasion.

"I wrote to my father telling him of the loss of the rifle he had gifted me."

It was Craven's turn to sigh in despair as he remembered how that had come to pass. The fine weapon had gone up in flames in Lisbon when their billets were set alight with them still inside. It might have been Timmerman who caused the fire, but it was he and his brother Hawkshaw who had caused the events led to that horrifying situation. It had caused them to have to flee the city for a while. Paget's woes with his father were also in large part Craven's fault, and he knew it. He felt his heart sink as he realised how much he had failed the young man as he went on.

"I left England on bad terms with my father, but I thought fond memories and a desire to do my duty might be enough to make one request."

"And what did you ask for?"

"A new rifle, so that I might continue to fulfil my duty and fight the French, Sir."

"And?"

"My father says he will not aid me further, not with a replacement rifle, nor in fact with any finances of any kind."

Craven huffed in frustration, but Paget was not done.

"He says that I will receive no more replies nor aid until I have resigned from the Salford Rifles and obtained a commission in a reputable regiment. He says I must reclaim my honour or be disowned." Paget came close to tears having said it aloud for the first time.

Craven looked to Matthys for help, and yet the Sergeant was nowhere to be seen, leaving him to resolve the mess himself.

"Much of this is my fault."

But Paget shook his head.

"I do not see my father here fighting for his country. He could have sought the command of a regiment. He could have led a brigade or even a division. He has the money and power to do so, and yet he sits comfortably at home whilst we fight." Tears streamed down his face, "Whatever your sins, Sir, you are ten times the man he will ever be, and I will not turn my back on my responsibilities like my father."

Craven was stunned and placed an arm around Paget's shoulders to embrace him tightly. He knew this was the moment that Paget truly landed in the same boat as the rest of them, for he was cut off from the wealth he had known all his life. Now all he had were the soldiers who fought beside him, the same as Craven.

"You would give up everything for us?"

"I am not giving up anything, Sir. I am doing my duty as a man, as a soldier, and as an Englishman."

Craven was close to tears himself as he was astonished by Paget's dedication to them all. And it would not go underappreciated, as the young Lieutenant had proven himself to be a most valuable asset both as a fighter and as a friend. Craven struggled to find any words for his appreciation of the Lieutenant, until he thought back to the letter that had started it all, and he finally spoke up.

"I came here to Portugal to make my fortune. I don't know if we can find it, nor replace a fraction of what you have lost, but I will try, but I will promise you this, I will get you that rifle."

"Thank you, Sir," sobbed Paget.

"James," replied Craven.

Paget smiled through his tears, for it was a great honour to be granted permission to use a commanding officer's first name, especially for such a young and junior officer. He couldn't imagine he ever would be able to, but the sentiment meant everything.

"This, all of this, it means the world to me. More than any wealth or status or approval ever could."

"I'll remind you of that fact when the money runs out," laughed Craven.

"The French have everything we could ever want, and we will take it from them at will," declared Paget sternly.

"That's the spirit," smiled Craven.

Paget looked confident in his words, and yet the letter and news evidently still weighed heavily on his mind.

"Tomorrow we will have some real soldiering to do," insisted Craven in an attempt to take his mind off of his woes.

"You think so, Sir?" Paget now asked excitedly.

"You heard the Major. He has work for us, and he knows just what we are good for."

"Yes, Sir," Paget smiled back at him.

"Be ready at first light."

Craven left the Lieutenant in better spirits than he had found him. He retired to Ferreira's position. The Portuguese Captain looked indifferent to their situation and was sitting beside Matthys.

"That was one of the bravest things you have ever done,"

whispered Matthys.

Craven hadn't realised anyone had been listening to his conversation with Paget and did not know how to respond to his comment.

"Perhaps we finally found your soft side," smiled Ferreira.

"We all need something to get us through this damned winter," admitted Craven.

"Spring will have a shit job for us tomorrow. So, you go off and cause trouble, and the rest of us must suffer the punishment," declared Ferreira.

"Aye, and you would have shared in the rewards, too, wouldn't you?"

"Of course," smirked Ferreira.

"Get some rest, whatever the Major has in store for us, I am sure it won't be easy."

* * *

Craven waited outside the largest house in the small Portuguese town in the bitter morning cold. It was hardly a lavish residence, and yet it was still far better than the rest of their billets. For a start it had a large stone fireplace from which smoke was arising, and Craven enviously imagined the warmth which would be enjoyed by those inside. Food and heat were seemingly all that mattered to the troops as they waited out the winter.

"Captain Craven!" a voice roared as he was called inside.

Hawkshaw, Paget, and Ferreira waited outside with anticipation. The waft of wood smoke upon entering and thick warm air was most inviting as Craven stepped inside and into a dining room which had been adapted into an officer's command post. Although it was not Major Spring sitting behind the table being used as a desk, for he was standing behind the officer who was a man Craven did not recognise.

"You are the rogue who stole from one of my officers, are you?" demanded the officer.

"I stole only from the French, Sir."

He knew that wasn't entirely true, and yet in this particular case it was, and he was not oblivious to how shallow a defence that was.

"Major Spring here tells me you are accused of stealing several turkeys and a sheep belonging to Captain Harding." The officer looked to Major Spring for confirmation.

"Indeed, though it must be noted that Captain Craven was only found in possession of a single pig, and nothing more."

"You would not find such a fine meal through any legitimate means here, and so a thief you are, Sir," declared the officer.

Craven did not even have the energy to fight the claim, as it was indeed true in so many ways.

"This is Colonel Rooke. The Colonel here has a problem with the French stealing supplies," declared Major Spring.

"Indeed, I need a thief to steal back what is rightfully ours!" Rooke laughed.

"Taking from the French is no problem for me, Sir."

"No, I suppose not, if only you could only take from the enemy. I know of your exploits, Captain. They say you are a great fighter, and Major Spring assures me the rumours are true, but I expect more of a soldier than for him to just fight. Honour and duty, Captain!"

"Yes, Sir," Craven answered wearily.

"I must leave you gentlemen for there is much to be done."

Spring then set out quickly. Rooke rested back in his chair and glared at Craven who didn't much like the Colonel's attitude, but he was in no position to protest over it.

"I know your sort, Captain. A ragged criminal thinking he can use that uniform to get away with murder and more," began Rooke.

"It's what I am paid to do, Sir."

"By God, it is not, Sir!" Rooke shot forward and slammed his fist on the table with a temper equal only to Wellington himself. He then sat back and sighed furiously.

"Captain Craven, you have gotten by in this army by achieving success and somehow expected that forgives all of your crimes. Your insubordination and your shameful conduct. That comes to an end, now!"

Craven said nothing. He had no respect for Rooke as a man who he knew nothing about and appeared to merely command from behind a desk. Even so, he knew saying anything would land him in even more trouble.

"Major Spring tells me the matter of the theft of the animals has been settled, but I do not consider it so. An officer does not thieve from another officer. But I have a problem of thieving myself. The French have taken valuable supplies, powder stores, muskets, and the like. Enough to equip a company, you see, and the lives of several of my men were lost in the process. I want those supplies back. Do you hear me?"

"Yes, Sir," replied Craven eagerly as it was just the sort of work which he was happy to conduct, and it was better than sitting idle.

"Major Spring tells me this is the kind of task you are perfectly suited to, Captain. Bring back what was taken, and I will consider the matter of your own theft to be closed."

"Yes, Sir."

"See the Lieutenant beyond that door, and he will outline everything we know."

Rooke pointed to the door dismissively as if he either didn't like Craven or didn't have any faith in him completing the mission. Perhaps both.

"Colonel," declared Craven before leaving the room.

Paget waited excitedly for news or anything to set his mind to as he paced anxiously back and forth outside.

"I think you expect too much," said Ferreira.

"Nonsense. If Major Spring has a job for us, then it is surely dangerous and exciting."

"All of this because of a single pig?" Hawkshaw asked exhaustedly.

"We both know Craven's offences extend far further than a single incident," replied Ferreira.

"And yet of this one the Captain was not even guilty, for how could he have stolen and cooked two turkeys and a sheep without any of us noticing?" Paget added.

They needn't wait any longer as Craven stormed out to join them.

"Well, Sir?" Paget asked.

"We have work to do." He walked on by and left them struggling to keep up.

"What sort of work, Sir?"

"I am going to find what the army has lost, and I'll need

twenty men to do it."

"I will eagerly accompany you, Sir.

Craven stopped as he made some quick decisions.

"All right, and Ferreira, you are with me, too. Find me seventeen more, crack shots, men you can rely on not to find more trouble than they must."

Ferreira raced on to gather the modest force as Craven turned to Hawkshaw. He could tell his brother's stomach for war had not returned.

"You have command whilst we are gone. There is still much to be done. We have fresh soldiers without any idea what it is really like out there. Train them and sweat them."

"Yes, Sir."

It was not long before they were on their way, travelling on foot with everything they needed on their backs. Every man wore a greatcoat and carried a blanket on his back. They were as well equipped for winter as they could be, and yet they knew any night under the stars would be a bitter one. Moxy and Ellis led the way as they utilised their tracking skills. Vicenta, Charlie, and Barros had joined them also.

"I see you did not select Birback," said Paget to Ferreira.

"That man is like a bull, and sometimes that is a most valuable quality, but not today."

The party laughed as they went on. Caffy and Amyn had also stayed back at camp.

"Sir, I have to wonder if we are being given much of a chance to succeed?"

Paget was looking upon their small numbers and also lamented the lack of his horse Augustus.

"This was so Colonel Rooke cannot lose."

"How so, Sir? I do not understand."

"He doesn't like me, and if this mission is the end of me, then it is at a small cost to the army. But if we succeed, it was with nothing risked."

"I am sure that is not true, Sir," replied Paget, but one glance to Ferreira showed the feeling was shared by the Portuguese Captain also.

He looked aghast at the prospect, and yet nobody else appeared shocked or surprised at all. And it then dawned on him that his own father would likely not care if he died, only that he did so without shaming his name. The parallels sent chills down his spine.

They marched on without seeing any signs of the enemy as they made their way across the frontier border where small bands of soldiers and Bandidos all existed in the sprawling and barren lands without any law and order at all. As the sun went down, the Captain ordered a fire to be started and nobody protested. The flames soon reached up for the skies and could be seen for miles all around.

"Does it not concern you, Sir? That we have so little defence or cover from any onlookers."

"Any bastard stupid enough to be out there now will be dead by morning." Craven said as he rubbed his hands together.

They went on for another two days like that, rarely seeing sight of any life and sustaining themselves on the modest rations they carried with them. At least there was drinking water in abundance, as it was not quite cold enough for all the streams and rivers to ice over permanently. Moxy had no trouble following the tracks of the enemy, and finally on the third day he brought them to a stop just after noon. They all knew something significant lay on the road ahead, or what little was left of the road. It was merely a filthy track for which the cold had at least hardened the ground, so they were not fighting through swamp-like conditions.

"Wait here."

Craven gestured for Ferreira to go forward with him. They moved up to Moxy and Ellis and found them looking down at a small village. There were no guards on duty, but they could see four wagons rolled into a partially collapsed building. The roof was barely still standing, but enough to give some shelter to the supplies which were still stacked up.

"That's it," declared Craven as he got a good look at the wagons which were full of powder kegs and crates of muskets. Although the horses pulling them were nowhere to be seen, "No sentries it seems. We are in luck."

"Why? How could they be so foolish?" Ferreira asked.

"They probably think no one is mad enough to go after them," smiled Moxy.

Craven smiled and nodded in agreement.

"How do you want to do this?" asked Ferreira.

"We can't wait for darkness. It will make our escape too dangerous. The time has to be now."

"In daylight, and with only twenty men?"

"Twenty, and the element of surprise, I'll take those odds," he admitted.

Craven could hear the clatter of equipment behind and turned back furiously to scold his comrades.

"Be quiet," he hissed.

But he soon realised the noise was not coming from the small party he had brought with him. He readied his rifle, anticipating trouble. The others soon followed as they saw the concern on his face and quickly understood the danger. Moxy lay flat on his back against the shallow verge and rested the muzzle of his rifle on his feet, ready to take a steady shot at whoever came over the ridge.

"Wishing you brought more men now?" Ferreira whispered.

Craven grimaced as he suspected they were about to be trapped with the enemy in front and behind. Yet those approaching finally came into view. They looked a ragged bunch, wrapped in a broad mix of clothing from British to French and civilian also, but the one leading them was unmistakeable.

"Timmerman?" Ferreira scoffed.

He led more than thirty scruffy but hardy-looking men where they stopped beside Paget. Only the Major came forward to finally take a knee before Craven.

"What are you doing here?"

"You are always there for your friends, Craven, and I intend to do the same."

Craven was suspicious but groaned in approval.

"We are here to retrieve British equipment. It's not for thieving."

"And anything French?"

"That is fair game," admitted Craven, but he looked uncomfortable.

"What is it?" Timmerman asked.

"I came here with a handful of soldiers so as to move quietly and not draw attention," he replied as he looked at the force which had now more than doubled in strength.

"You'll be glad to have my boys when the shooting starts."

"If we play this right, there won't be any shooting."

"A quiet Craven mission?" Timmerman chuckled at the prospect.

Ferreira shrugged in begrudging agreement. A gasp rang out from behind them a little further along the road where it descended into the town. Craven looked around to see two French soldiers with a look of bewilderment and shock.

"Shit," muttered Craven.

CHAPTER 4

For a moment the two Frenchmen did not recognise what they were looking upon as Craven and his ragtag party stared back, but they soon recognised British uniforms and weapons and turned to run for help. They did not have a musket between them, as if never expecting to find any trouble. They were only wearing their small briquet short swords for protection from wild animals and the local population. Moxy quickly repositioned onto the ridge and took aim with his rifle.

"No, you'll alert the whole damned town." Craven threw down his rifle and pack and ran after them.

Timmerman did the same, drawing out a long and narrow brutal-looking stiletto dagger whilst Craven already had his sword in hand. They raced on after the Frenchmen as they fled rapidly. Ferreira and the others took up position along the roadside with their rifles at the ready as they watched the near silent chase.

After a while, one of the Frenchman cried out as loudly as his lungs would allow. But it did not carry far in the windy conditions, and Timmerman's dagger soon put an end to his cries. The blade was launched from over ten yards away and embedded in the man's back, causing him to collapse down onto the road.

His friend did not even hesitate upon seeing the other fall as he ran on. The Frenchman was wrapped in just as much heavy clothing as Craven, and yet the burden was on the Captain to close the distance as the man cried out in an attempt to get help. Craven sighed and cursed to himself as the painful memories of his loss to Nooth during Mathewson's gruelling and punishing challenges. He thought it stupid that he needed to beat a swordsman in a running race, but now Mathewson's challenges did not seem so ridiculous, but Craven would not stop cursing the old fencing master, nonetheless. However, the painful memory was a good motivator to give it everything he had, and his fitness and strength was significantly improved now as he soared on forwards. Soon enough he was quickly closing the distance.

The panicked Frenchman kept peering over his shoulder and soon realised he could not outrun Craven. And so he finally stopped, drew out his short sword, and prepared to defend himself. Craven did not slow down and approached like a galloping cavalryman. Normally, he would never take such a risk, but time was of the essence, and he had to finish his opponent quickly. He watched his enemy carefully to see every small motion of the man's sword and follow each change in direction of his blade as he rapidly closed the last few paces. He nimbly directed his own sword perfectly into the path of his opponent's so that it was carried away before the two crashed together, and he dealt a brutal left hook into the man's jaw. The Frenchman staggered back, and in his dazed confusion, Craven lunged after him. He plunged the point of his sword into the Frenchman's chest. The man fell back from the blade and drew his last few breaths as he died on the cold damp road.

Craven looked back to Timmerman with relief that they had succeeded in preventing the enemy from learning of their presence. The silence which followed was a welcome relief, but it was soon broken by the violent clang of a bell. Someone in the town had raised the alarm.

"Shit," muttered Craven as he realised all hell was about to break loose.

"On me!" he roared at the top of his voice.

All of those who had marched with him came charging down the road, and Timmerman's ragtag bunch were intermingled with them. Craven had no time to protest as he ran on towards the carts.

"You're really going to keep on with this?" Ferreira cried in horror that they had not fled at the first sign of trouble.

"We came here for those wagons, and I'll be damned if I am leaving without them!"

It was a dirty shallow road which led them down into the village. As they dropped down into it, and the ground opened up before them, they realised it was a far larger and more sprawling settlement than had been visible from the approach road. The bell still rang violently, but a shot from Moxy soon silenced it, not that it would make any difference now. There was not a single person in the valley who could not have heard the panicked warning bell.

They ran on as a rabble, more reminiscent of a wild Celtic warband than a unit of disciplined professional soldiers. A Frenchman rushed out from one doorway and hurried to ready his musket. Craven did not break stride. He sprinted into the man, drove a knee into his groin, and delivered a devastating hook at the side of the soldier's head with the ward iron of his sword. The Frenchman collapsed and was out cold instantly as his musket fell to the ground. Craven continued to lead the way, having barely lost a few seconds.

Several more Frenchmen appeared in doorways and one on a rooftop ahead as they ran on. A few shots rang out, but more from the mob of ragtag soldiers who ran onwards. The wagons were soon in view and Craven darted up to them. He was panting heavily now. They all were, for the tense situation weighed heavily on top of the rapid physical exertion.

"Horses?" he asked as he looked for any sign of them.

"Here!" Ferreira shouted, who was more eager to leave the place than any of them.

Craven turned to bark his orders when out of the corner of his eye he caught a glimpse of movement. He turned in time to see a soldier swing a pioneer's axe downward at him. It was as if the man was trying to take his head clean off in an execution upon the scaffold. He leapt aside, and the axe smashed onto the ground just two inches from his foot. He then drove his sword into the wielder's chest, finishing him instantly. Paget sighed in relief, seemingly more worried about the close call than Craven was, but the truth was the Captain had no time to worry about it, and he rushed to the edge of the street to assess the situation.

"Get those wagons ready to move!" he roared as he raced away.

"You heard the Captain!" Paget called out, showing Timmerman's rank no respect at all. Their old enemy did not protest as he merely seemed to be revelling in the chaos. Craven soon came running back with a look of concern on his face.

"The French are coming."

"How many?" Paget asked.

"All of them!" Craven said as he rushed past to see to the wagons and hurry the men along.

"Stand and fight," Timmerman said to him as approached. Craven sighed at the prospect.

"What? You don't have the stomach for it?"

"I just don't want to fight a battle we can't win."

"Bullshit, that is not the Craven I know. The enemy advancing on us are not expecting a fight. They were not ready for it. They are expecting to run us out of town, running in fear from them, but what if we did not do that?"

"He has a point." Ferreira was tying down the harness onto a horse before one of the wagons. Craven stopped for a moment. He knew he had to think fast, and that it was a risk no matter what his decision.

"Your boys will stand with mine?" he finally asked.

"We will," replied Timmerman as he committed to standing in the line himself.

Craven stepped out from the ruined structure and into the street once more where a number of their modest force awaited the enemy, sheltered as best they could in doorways and at the corners of buildings. Moxy and Ellis were lying prone on the roof of a short building on the far side of the street.

"We send enough lead down that street, and they won't keep coming," insisted Timmerman.

Craven nodded in agreement. He liked the idea, despite how little he trusted Timmerman and his associates, but time was running out, and he could hear the clatter of French soldiers approaching.

"Form up! Three ranks!" Craven quickly took measure of the narrow street. Many looked surprised, with Moxy not wanting to move and many of Timmerman's men looking to him.

"You heard the Captain," insisted Timmerman.

"Three ranks!" Paget cried out in confirmation.

At more than fifteen wide the rank was shoulder to shoulder and stretched the full width of the road, but despite their ragtag appearance, the mix of troops were quickly formed up as though ready to fight on a great open battlefield. They could hear the clatter of equipment and cries of the French as they approached on the street ahead, and it would not be long before they appeared at the bend.

"Front rank, kneel!" Craven ordered.

They dropped down.

"Make ready!"

The muskets and rifles of all were moved from the shoulder and brought to full cock. It brought a shiver down Paget's spine, as it was a reminder of the times they had marched before the enemy on several great battlefields where tens of thousands of soldiers had clashed. Seconds later, the French came into view. Dozens of infantrymen and officers, and even some dismounted cavalrymen were amongst them. It was a disorganised rabble, though not nearly as ragged and scruffy looking as the British and Portuguese troops.

"Present!"

The French troops looked stunned, but they only hesitated for a brief second before continuing their advance as if somehow the charge would be enough to make their adversaries run rather than stand and fire.

"Fire!" Craven cried.

He fired one barrel of his pistol down the narrow street as fifty muskets and rifles ignited all at once in a deafening volley in the narrow and crowded street. They lost sight of the enemy instantly as they were engulfed by a cloud of acrid powder smoke, but the sound of weapons being loaded soon echoed out as every man readied a second shot without any command having to be given, for not one of them was a common line infantryman. They were all accustomed to fighting as skirmishers and fighting using their own initiative. Craven merely watched as the powder began to dissipate. He could hear the sound of the enemy approaching as well as the cries of the wounded. The fog of powder smoke lit up as several shots were fired through it from the French, but not one shot found its mark. They were firing blind and were disorientated as they coughed and spluttered and struggled on.

"Give them another!"

The smoke cloud lifted a little, and they could see the silhouettes of some of those who approached and the bodies of many who had fallen.

"Make ready!" he called out once more, "Present! Fire!"

This time it was their turn to fire into the cloud of powder smoke, but with a volley of muskets down the narrow street, and with the faint shadows of Frenchmen ahead, they could not fail to miss. For a moment the air all around them become hot, and some of them even sweat a few drops as the volley of muskets lit up the scene, once more engulfing them all in a blinding and intoxicating fog. They lost sight of the enemy completely as the situation only grew worse. Once more the sound of cartridges being torn open and ramrods scraping along barrels echoed out as Craven hurried to reload his double-barrelled pistol, which he had never done so quickly before. He clutched two cartridges together in his fist, biting both balls off together and pouring down both barrels together. He was ramming home when the cloud of powder smoke began to dissipate.

The scene fell eerily quiet as those loading were either finished or froze as he did to look upon the devastation before them. The street was littered with the bodies of the French dead, and those on their feet were burned, bloodied, and their will to go on was entirely broken. Craven took a deep breath in astonishment before finishing the loading of his weapon as the others did the same. They were ready to give another devastating volley, but there was no need, as they watched the Frenchmen turn back or collapse where they were standing.

"Shall we finish them off?" Timmerman asked.

Craven was tempted, for they were the enemy after all, but he imagined Matthys standing beside him, judging him silently with just his eyes, and he shook his head.

"Let's get what we came for."

The neatly dressed lines quickly collapsed as the troops scattered to ready the horses and wagons. Others took up defensive positions in readiness for another attack. Craven remained where he had commanded from and watched the enemy wounded like a hawk.

"You showed mercy, Sir?" Paget asked.

"They are done. We don't need to make them suffer any

further."

"I am surprised to hear you say so of the French, Sir."

Craven sighed and nodded in agreement.

"I know what it's like to be kicked when you are down."

"Yes, Sir."

Timmerman joined them also with a giant smile on his face, though they were still very suspicious of his presence.

"Just as well I came," he declared.

"You've never shied away from a fight nor the killing. Problem is you were never too fussy about which side you were killing."

"Don't sell yourself short, Craven. I didn't look for all Englishmen to kill, just two specific ones," he smirked.

The memories made Paget shiver, but Craven could not help but find it funny after all they had been through. He was more surprised that Timmerman had come at all, and even more so that he had managed to maintain a disciplined force through the battle. It was hard for him to hate Timmerman, as he saw plenty of himself in his old rival, and they had shared so much history together that he almost felt like a friend now.

"There must be hundreds more Frenchmen in this place, thousands even. They will be along shortly," declared Paget in concern as he looked at the French dead and wounded.

"Undoubtedly. Then let's be on our way, shall we?"

Craven left Timmerman to watch the enemy as he went to check on the state of the wagons. He heard a heavy creaking noise as one was pulled out into the daylight. There was no doubt it was heavily laden. The two horses driving it were straining their muscles to drag it a few paces, and the wheels and axles complained loudly at the weight they held up.

"Come on, let's see what we have, shall we?"

Nobody complained as they were all curious, despite expecting to find only a stack of infantryman's muskets. The humble Brown Bess, or Land Pattern Musket which did so much of the hard work in the war, but to Craven and his comrades were not the least bit intriguing.

Sergeant Barros reached for a spade on the wagon and drove it into the lid of the nearest box before prising it open.

"Well, I'll be damned," said Moxy as he looked down from the roof where he had been before. He was now marvelling at the contents of the box.

"It's no wonder the Colonel wanted these wagons." Craven reached in and pulled out a pristine and brand-new pattern 1800 infantry rifle. It was commonly referred to as the Baker rifle. Craven had not seen such a perfect condition rifle in several years. It had evidently never been issued as there was not a mark on the woodwork. It was a handy little rifle, shorter than those his men used by their rifle militia days, and yet no less accurate. Moxy looked on enviously at the beautiful weapons, but then instantly felt guilty. He set his eyes on his own rifle and ran his hand down the stock as if to apologise for looking upon another with such desire.

"Baker rifles, Sir? A mighty treasure and a rare sight," said Paget excitedly.

He was right. Only the rifle regiments carried the coveted Baker rifle, which put the Brown Bess to shame in any tests of shooting skill. In practice, the Baker rifle had become more prolific than intended, with some Line regiments procuring them for their Light companies, and even some cavalry regiments, too. But the Lieutenant was still correct, they were a rare sight.

Even the Portuguese Caçadores could only supply certain companies with the Baker rifle, and not all of Ferreira's soldiers were lucky enough to have gotten their hands on one. And those they did have were now several years old, having served a hard life on campaign, nothing like the crisp new beauty of the one in his hands. Craven looked down at Paget to see he still only had his pistol and sword with which to fight the enemy. He was reminded of the tragic loss of the Lieutenant's treasured rifle and the fateful letter he had received upon asking for a replacement from his father.

"Here!" He tossed the gleaming new rifle at Paget who only just managed to catch it in time. He looked stunned as he held the weapon at arm's reach and admired it.

"It is a fine weapon indeed."

It was a common soldier's weapon and nothing as refined and ornate as the one his father had given him, but it was of fine quality, and he was well aware of just how effective and efficient a killer it could be.

"Keep it," insisted Craven.

"Sir?" Paget asked in amazement.

"That rifle will do more work in your hands than wherever it was intended."

It was pure speculation, but he had seen Paget make some impressive shots in the past years, and he was glad to see the Lieutenant properly armed once more.

"We're ready!"

Ferreira personally led another of the wagons out into the street and climbed up onto the seat in readiness to depart. They could hear the cries of French troops as they made their way through the town to fend off raiding troops.

"Let's not outstay our welcome!" Craven roared as more of the wagons were dragged out from cover. There were eight in total, all well laden, and the seat of each could only fit three men at a push. Craven jumped onto the back of the one Ferreira had stepped onto. The rest of troops clambered onto the crates and barrels, precariously balancing themselves as best they could.

"Lead the way, Captain," ordered Craven to his Portuguese comrade.

Vicenta leapt on board beside Craven whilst Paget, Charlie, and Ellis took the seat of the next wagon. Ferreira took the reins and spurred the horses on. The huge, spoked wheels creaked as they lurched forward. It was a bumpy ride but compared to the primitive locally produced Portuguese carts with their solid wheels and lack of independent axles, it was surprisingly comfortable. Craven looked back from the top of the heavily laden wagon to see all seven of the others following on. It couldn't have been more of a success. For they had taken back the supplies without a single casualty, but as he gazed at his comrades, he caught sight of Timmerman looking back at him. He tipped his hat in appreciation, for which he never thought he would see the day.

"I thought when he showed up it was to take what we had come for," replied Ferreira as he gazed back.

"He may yet," admitted Craven. Even so, it was hard to not feel appreciation for the Major's efforts.

They were soon climbing the road from where they had descended into the town and looked back to see a hive of activity. French troops were swarming through the town looking for them. It was a relief to be well on their way as they passed the bodies of the two Frenchmen who they had first encountered. They turned a bend in the road and rode on into a wood.

"What the hell is that?" Ferreira asked.

The smile on Craven's face vanished as he looked forward. A troop of French light cavalry on the road ahead were coming straight for them. There was no way off the road. There were dense trees and foliage on either side of them and no other roads, nor could they turn around.

"Go through them!" Don't stop!"

Ferreira looked concerned but knew there was no other choice, and he quickly spurred the horses on to go faster. "We can't outrun them!"

"I don't mean to. We will go through them like a battering ram," declared Craven as he looked back at the train of heavily laden wagons.

The French drew swords and made their advance, but as they closed the distance, Sergeant Barros took a shot and knocked down the officer leading them. Craven nodded in appreciation.

"Here!"

Ferreira handed the Sergeant his rifle so that he could take a second shot without having to reload. Barros targeted another officer, but with the rattling of the wagons he did not get a clean shot, and the ball skimmed the Frenchman's arm, but it was still enough to make him drop his sword. The French cavalry quickly realised the wagons were not going to stop, and they parted at the centre as they leapt from the road onto the slippery embankments either side. Craven turned back to the others to relay one last order.

"Give 'em hell!"

He swung his sword about in the air and turned back to the enemy. They were within pistol shot now, and two of the cavalrymen shot at him directly. One shot whizzed past his head, and the other struck the wooden crate he was resting on. He returned fire, hitting one of his attackers square in the chest and shooting the hat off of the other.

"Not bad!" Ferreira laughed as he drew out his sabre to defend himself and continued to drive the horses on.

Craven tossed his pistol down amongst the crates so that he could hold on with his left hand as he leant out of the edge and hacked at the first French cavalryman he could reach. The Frenchman parried it but was run through by Vicenta a second later before he could reply to the second attack.

They gave the cavalrymen a taste of their own medicine, riding on by as though they themselves were the cavalry. Musket, rifle, and pistol fire rang out; those on the wagons firing at point-blank range as the wagons clattered on past the cavalrymen. Many were blown from their saddles. Timmerman reached out well over the edge of his wagon and hacked down at one sergeant, slashing him from shoulder to waist with a devastating blow.

Again and again shots rang out as Paget looked back to see each wagon run the gauntlet and unload a savage collection of shots and blows. His face lit up.

"It's just like Trafalgar!"

It was true. For they had parted the enemy and run the length of both sides, smashing them as they did, just like the opening of that triumphant sea battle. Steel clashed, and the cavalrymen became engulfed in a cloud of smoke as they tried in vain to fight back. Soon enough all the wagons had gone through them, leaving the troopers in a ragged state with many on the ground or slumped over their horses. They were shattered and with no willpower left to go on as they made no attempt to pursue the wagons. The battering ram had worked just as intended, for their morale was shattered as badly as their bodies. Cheers rang out from the soldiers atop the wagons as they rode on in triumph, and yet Ferreira shook his head and sighed in relief at how close a run it had been.

"You okay?" Craven asked.

"I hate to say it, but Timmerman really saved us, didn't he?"

"Yes, he did," smiled Craven.

CHAPTER 5

The clash of singlesticks rang out as Nooth and five other men practiced in the cold crisp afternoon air, stripped to the waist so that they could only stay warm by keeping up the fight with great vigour. Amyn and Joze watched with great amazement as they clashed back and forth, with every man amongst them practicing throughout the day. Many were bruised and battered by the exertions, but it was a welcome distraction from the monotony of army life as they endured the winter with nothing else to do.

"Good, good!" Matthys roared as he oversaw them before bringing them to a halt and giving them a new exercise.

"You see that wall? You three up against it, you are now defending with your backs against the wall. For sometimes footwork cannot save you and you have nowhere to run!"

Nooth and two other men took up their positions against the side of a large barn whilst Matthys huddled around with the three attackers to give his commands before stepping back.

"Ready! Begin!"

A war cry rang out as the three attackers sprinted forward to attack those against the wall without any intention of keeping distance like a fencer or a duellist would. One was struck on the way in and stopped, but the other two got to grappling range, disarming one of the attackers. The final man was locked in combat with Nooth as punches were thrown, and they fell down to the ground as they fought for control over the two weapons in between punching at any opening they could. They paused upon the abrupt arrival of several horses and looked up to see Colonel Rooke with two of his staff officers. Matthys called them to attention, but Rooke didn't care for it as he went on.

"What unit is this?" he demanded.

"Salford Rifles, Sir," replied Matthys.

Rooke rolled his eyes and shook his head in disappointment.

"What is the meaning of these silly games?" Rooke asked Matthys as the most senior soldier he could see and the only one who had answered his question.

"The men train for battle, Sir."

"Battle? These men play like children with sticks and rolling about the floor like fools. Battle is fought in a line of brave soldiers, or from the saddle with steel in hand. I will not have you wasting time on these silly little games!"

"Sir, I must tell you that these games prepare our men for battles we have fought many times," insisted Matthys.

"I will not be told what war is by a so-called sergeant in a band of brigands who is somehow allowed to fight with this army, do you hear me?" Rooke snarled at him with complete distain.

Matthys was appalled by the Colonel's words, but he was in no position to refute them.

"Sergeant, if your men will not conduct and exercise themselves as soldiers, then I will not treat them as such. The entrance road East to this town is in a ruinous state. Put a work party together. Every man I can see here and another ten from your so-called Salford Rifles. Gather some shovels and get to work! I'll have the Lieutenant here show you the way and keep a keen eye on you."

"Yes, Sir."

Rooke tutted in disgust with them before turning his horse about to leave.

"You heard the Colonel. We have work to do!"

Matthys was as disgusted as the rest of them, but orders were orders, and he would see them done as he yelled for several others to join them. They marched on as a rabble, picking up tools from a pile at the roadside as they went on by. Amyn did not complain as he joined them.

"I have seen many of these men fight, great warriors all of them, and those who have joined this winter will soon be so, too," he declared as he walked beside Matthys.

"Yes, indeed," groaned Matthys.

"Why then does that man treat us like criminals?"

"The Colonel does not appreciate Captain Craven and his means of conducting war."

"Does he not get results?"

"Without a doubt, but they are not always so clear and easy for all to see."

"We are wasted here."

"That much is true, but we must wait out this winter like

everyone else, and then we will go on doing what we do best."

They work detail was led to a road with deep holes and collapsing sides. Several soldiers struggled to move a cart that had dropped into a deep muddy rut.

"On me!" Matthys shouted. He and the others gathered about the cart and put their weight and muscle into it. The cart lurched a little and finally lifted out of the hole and became free.

"There is your work. Get to it!" yelled the Lieutenant who had been sent to watch over them.

Matthys hadn't asked his name, for he didn't care to know it. They put their tools to work, and soon enough the discontentment amongst them over the menial task faded away. In truth it was appreciated to have something to do rather than nothing, especially in the harsh winter. They had been at the work for a little over an hour when Matthys stretched upright and wiped his brow to take a brief rest. He noticed a wagon train approaching, heavily laden and bristling with armed soldiers.

"It's the Captain!" Joze yelled.

Craven and his modest selection of soldiers had been gone almost a week and some were starting to worry. The frontier lands were a dangerous place, and as much as Matthys had faith in Craven, the Captain was not invincible.

"Is that…Timmerman?" Joze asked.

"Yes, it is."

Several horses rode up behind them, and they turned back. It was the Colonel coming to ensure they were hard at work. It was hard for him to complain when he got a look at the results of their hard work, and anyway his attention was soon drawn to Craven, for whom he had been awaiting news. Ferreira drew up the triumphant column beside the work detail as several of them leapt off and mingled with their comrades, sharing the stories of their adventures.

"Have you returned with my supplies?" Rooke asked in spite of being able to see with his own eyes that they had, and yet he wanted to hear it from Craven.

"See for yourself, Colonel," replied Craven.

Rooke gestured for the Lieutenant he had sent to watch over the work detail to now inspect the wagons. The man dismounted before climbing up onto the wagon beside Craven.

"Well?"

"Sir, these are indeed our supplies, but one of the crates has been opened," declared the Lieutenant.

"Has it, by God?" He rode up beside the cart and stood up in his stirrups to peer over the edge and get a look for himself. The Lieutenant pulled the lid away to reveal the crate of Baker rifles with a single weapon missing.

"Where is it?" Rooke demanded.

"All of this, and you care about one rifle?"

"One rifle, a hundred rifles, the matter is the same. Captain!" Rooke shouted angrily.

Craven sighed and controlled his anger, changing tack to see if he could justify it in another way.

"We had to fight our way out of a French town against infantry and cavalry, and that rifle was needed."

"And now it is not!"

Craven dropped his head in despair.

"Here it is, Sir," Paget's voice rang out.

"Keep it," ordered Craven.

"You will not, Sir."

"One rifle for a man who risked his life to get you all of

this?"

"Risking your life is what you are paid to do, Captain. It is what we are all paid to do. And anyway, an officer has no need of a common soldier's weapon."

Rooke gestured for his Lieutenant to take the weapon, but it broke Craven's heart to see what its loss meant to Paget, who offered it up because of his devotion to duty. But he clutched onto the weapon until the very last second, not wanting to give it up, until finally it was snatched from his hands, and the brief joy he had gotten from the gift was snatched away with it.

"Off with all of you. These wagons are now the possession of the Army once more!"

Rooke glared angrily at Timmerman and the others who were still straddling the wagons and their loads. Timmerman groaned as he slid off the side, and his bad attitude clearly caught the attention of Rooke.

"Your tone, Sir, it is unacceptable."

Timmerman smiled in response and gave him no attention.

"What is your name, Mister. For I should know the one who disrespects me so!"

Timmerman stopped and turned to face off against the Colonel. He looked calm, but anyone who knew the Major knew he was simmering and soon to boil over.

"Why? What are you going to do with it?"

"Damn you, Sir. I should have you put on a charge and reported to your commanding officer!"

"Be my guest," he snarled in response.

Rooke drew his sword and rode forward, stopping only a few paces before Timmerman as he tried to intimidate him, but the Major calmly held his ground and did not even reach for a weapon. He was cocky and calm, but also arrogant, qualities which rubbed the Colonel up entirely the wrong way.

"I will have your name, Sir," he demanded.

"Timmerman," he replied calmly.

Rooke's face turned to stone as he realised his mistake.

"Major Sir Alexander Vandertray Timmerman," he bellowed for all to hear.

"My apologies." Rooke sheathed his sword and turned away.

Timmerman's men laughed at the scene, only adding to the Colonel's humiliation, but he dared not say another word as he rode on. He stopped beside Craven, hoping to reassert himself, and yet he was clearly embarrassed by his own humiliation.

"Good work, Captain," he said before riding on without another word as troops arrived to drive the wagons away. It was Paget who watched them leave with the most sadness, for with them went the rifle which he rightfully deserved and had been gifted.

"We will get you another, I promise you that. One which no one can ever take away," pledged Craven.

The look of despair on Paget's face was not at all unique, for as Craven looked around, he could see the whole army felt the same. They were exhausted and anxious but also bored and restless. The discontent was everywhere to see.

"Welcome back," said Matthys.

Craven nodded in appreciation.

"What has that idiot got you doing here?" Craven looked at the tools in their hands and their dirty appearance.

"The Colonel does not approve of our training methods."

"No? Well, I will decide what is best for the Salfords."

"I am not sure the Colonel will agree."

"To hell with the spineless bastard. He got what he wanted."

Craven watched Paget walk away with Charlie doing her best to console him.

"A rough time out there?"

"Hardly, it's not the battle that gets him down, but the one he is still fighting."

"Is there something I should know?"

"Honestly, I don't have the heart to tell you."

* * *

Craven watched Nooth lead ten men on a course he had set up. They advanced across rough terrain and pretended to fire as they moved, covering one another and working as the skirmishers they had trained to be. Yet they did not burn any powder, for it could not be spared. The Captain looked weary of it and turned away, looking out into the distance as if in a dream. A few moments later Nooth returned to his side, having completed the course.

"Are we boring you, Captain?"

"Yes, you are," admitted Craven, no longer having any patience. Colonel Rooke's bad attitude and Paget's lost rifle still weighed heavily on his mind, and he was exhausted by the perpetual training. Nooth cursed angrily. Craven looked entirely disinterested and that angered Nooth further.

"If you are bored by all of this, how do you think we feel?"

"Easy now," insisted Matthys.

But Nooth would not back down.

"All we do is train, harder and more often than anyone in the army. We are ready, and we have been since we arrived in this damned country."

"You think you are ready to face the French?" Craven smiled back at him.

"Of course, we are, and there is fighting to be done, even whilst this winter persists. You got your crack at the French going after those supplies, what about us, when will we get our chance?"

Several of the men who had volunteered together with Nooth stepped up to support him. Even Quicks and his friends joined him, despite them having no love for one another.

"You want a crack at the French, do you?"

"Yeah!" roared the small crowd.

Craven smiled as he looked to Matthys who shook his head as he could see what was coming.

"Gather your equipment. We move out in one hour."

"To find the enemy?" Nooth asked suspiciously, assuming it was a trick.

"I will take you out onto that frontier. A barren land where there is far more to worry about than just the French. I will lead you out there, and we will see if you are ready," replied Craven sternly, as if he had no faith in their abilities and was calling their bluff.

But Nooth could hardly believe their luck as the group began to cheer and jump for joy.

"Well, go on then!" Craven hollered at them.

They quickly vanished to go and gather everything they needed to march and to fight. Craven waited for Matthys' inevitable condemnation.

"Are you doing this for you or for them?"

Craven looked surprised. It was not the approach he expected his pious friend to take.

"You don't approve?" he smiled.

"Putting them in a little danger before the chaos of the spring ensues is no bad thing. I just want to know you are doing it for the right reasons."

"Honestly? I am sick of Nooth's belly aching. It is time he was put before the enemy and we see what kind of man he really is, and the same for the rest of them."

"And if it costs lives?"

"Then better we find out our strength now and not when we march into Spain," replied Craven coldly.

Matthys nodded in agreement, it being a hard truth he could not deny.

"Just promise me you will not get a man killed to prove a point?"

"You know me better than to ask that."

Matthys looked ashamed of himself for having asked it.

"I'm sorry, but we are all tense after months of inactivity," admitted Matthys.

"I'd say I'm surprised to hear you admit it, but nothing surprises me now. Timmerman came out onto the frontier to assist us, and risked everything to do so, can you believe that?"

"And there was nothing to gain from it?"

"I can't see how. He fought with us, under my command and in an orderly conduct," replied Craven in disbelief.

"Men can change. He might be the last man I would expect it from, but I hold out hope and pray for it every day. Perhaps my prayers have been answered."

"He can certainly be a useful weapon at the right moment," admitted Craven.

"He handled the Colonel."

"I am starting to think the Colonel doesn't like us."

The two men laughed together, remembering how the Colonel ran with his tail between his legs upon realising who Timmerman was.

"The Colonel certainly won't approve of us departing without orders," replied Matthys.

"I'm done taking orders from that fool. He can take it up with Wellington. I did what Spring asked of me. We are done."

"But I don't believe the Colonel is done with us."

"Then we'll cross that bridge when we come to it."

CHAPTER 6

All the Salfords were formed up, and they now totalled almost three hundred soldiers. Many were the militia who had joined them under Gamboa's watch. British volunteers and thieves recruited from the streets were standing beside veteran warriors, and yet they all wore the same red jacket, except Ferreira's Caçadores who would not give up the brown jackets they wore with such pride. They were in the minority now, despite once making up the majority of Craven's ragtag bunch of fighters. It had been an exhausting time, doing nothing and with so little certainty of what the new year would bring, but gathered together the excitement began to build. They were on a slight incline, with Craven on the high ground and able to see them all. He looked around with pride and almost disbelief of where he found himself as they keenly awaited his address. He looked to Matthys to find his old friend nodding in approval before he took a deep breath and began.

"When we came here to Portugal, it was to help in the battle waging across all of Portugal and Spain. I am sure you have all read or heard the news, how can you not? The armies and fortresses of Spain collapse day after day, and soon enough I imagine the French will have all of Spain. I have no doubt the people of Spain will keep on fighting in any way they can, but this army we have, Wellington's army, it is all that stands between the French taking it all. One day soon we will have our orders to march with Wellington to decide the fate of the whole Iberian Peninsula, and when that day comes, I would have every man here ready for whatever comes next. I will not have the first time any of you see a French soldier be before tens of thousands of the bastards!"

A cheer and laughter rang out, but he soon called for silence. He pointed East towards Spain.

"Out there are the French. They scout the ground; they probe our lines for weaknesses. They hunt and terrorise the locals who stand against them. If you march East, then soon enough you will bump into the French, and that is just what I intend to do. Not with a handful of soldiers, but with all of you. I mean to look for trouble, and I certainly intend to find it!"

An excited cheer rang out as they waved their hats in the air and whistled and clapped. Craven looked back to his closest friends who awaited his orders.

"Let's do this." He turned and led the way forward to a cheer from the troops.

"Into column, prepare to march!" Hawkshaw shouted the order.

The orders were relayed onwards, but they all knew what they had to do as they went forward, forming up as they went on. They had only gotten two hundred yards when Colonel Rooke rode up to address them and came alongside Craven.

"What are you doing, Captain?"

"Taking my men East."

"I have given no such order to do so!"

"I answer only to Lord Wellington and Major Spring. I work for them."

"Major Spring seconded you and your men to my command."

"I have seen no such command. The Major asked me to help you return articles which were taken by the enemy, a task which I completed in full, and until such time as the Major returns, I will go on with my duty and follow the orders of Lord Wellington himself."

Rooke looked furious as he gave up the fight and stopped his horse to watch them march away, uncertain as to how the threat of Wellington's name might be used against him.

"That won't be the end of it," declared Matthys as he marched behind Craven.

"No, I am sure it won't be, but I won't have our men waste away under his orders for another day."

"And when we return?"

"Another bridge we will cross when we reach it."

Craven smiled as he stepped out of line but kept pace as he turned to walk backwards. He saw Rooke's disapproving expression for himself as they marched on. He soon rejoined the column with an even greater smile on his face.

"Are you sure it is wise to make an enemy of the Colonel, Sir?" Paget asked.

"That bastard was my enemy before we ever met. It's men

like that who will get you killed just to prove a point."

"And what point is that, Sir?"

"That one is a mystery known only to them," admitted Craven.

They continued to march out along the road many of them had so recently been working on to repair. Now a new selection of poor fellows was at it in their stead. Soon enough they were in open country and away from all the bustle of army cantonments. It was a breath of fresh air, quite literally, the fresh cool breeze a welcome experience. The smell of thousands of soldiers living together was a uniquely awful assault on the senses.

"What is the plan?" Matthys asked Craven.

"Just as I said."

"You are going to look for trouble and hope you find it, Sir?" Paget asked in amazement.

"Is a plan not allowed to be so simple?"

"Well, no, Sir, but I am not sure what is to be achieved. I thought we did not look for fights which need not be fought?"

"Whoever said that? Because I am sure it was not me."

Matthys grimaced and nodded in agreement, for he had often had to drag Craven away from needless violence or the path towards it, and yet he did not stand in the way this time.

"Then this is nothing but a Jolly, Sir?"

"Far from it. Nooth and many of the new recruits believe they are ready to face the enemy, and they need to be shown why they are not."

Paget thought back to his first experiences of battle and how terrifying it was.

"There is a first time for everything, I suppose," he

muttered.

"Yes, and I would know how they would respond to adversity before my life truly depended on it."

"Is that time not now if we march to face the enemy?"

"Perhaps. We'll see."

"Then what security is there if they are not up to the task, Sir?"

"That is what you are here for."

Paget smiled. It was deeply comforting to know he had the faith of the Captain in such a situation, and Matthys smiled to see Craven show some kindness to the young man as he continued to lift his spirits. Matthys had never been so proud of his old friend who continued to surprise him in the ways he always wished he would but did not know if he ever would.

They marched on through the day with morale remaining high as they searched for the enemy, but it was soon time to make camp. The fires were lit, and the troops settled in for a brisk night as they chatted enthusiastically about the days to come. Ferreira sat beside Craven and was deep in thought.

"You worry about the New Year?"

Ferreira nodded in agreement.

"You have seen the news. It will not be long before we stand alone against the armies of France, and as far as I hear it, they grow stronger every day."

"Not by a quarter as much as one would expect. If Napoleon was serious about taking Portugal, he would march down here with the largest army ever created and trample us into the damned ground."

"Then why does he not?"

"I don't know, how could I? Perhaps he doesn't think we

are any great threat?"

Ferreira laughed at that.

"Never underestimate an enemy, isn't that what you always say?"

"Absolutely. Napoleon will regret leaving this country to us, for in time we will take everything from him."

"I hope you are right, because all I see is the French winning great victories and replenishing their losses."

Craven shrugged as the politics and logistics of the war were far beyond him. Yet as they fell silent, the tantalising and mouth-watering waft of cooking meat passed their noses and made Craven's stomach rumble. He looked around for the source of it as it was the last thing he expected to experience out on the march in winter.

"That is no simple meal," he said as he got up.

He looked over to one of the other fires. An animal on a spit was cooking over it. He shook his head in disbelief and raced over to see for himself. Ferreira and Matthys followed him. They arrived to find a plump bird roasting over the fire and Quicks attending to it.

"What is it you have there?" Craven enquired.

"Turkey," he replied with a wicked smile. Craven looked over to another fire beside it with a second turkey roasting atop it.

"Captain Harding's two turkeys?" Craven gasped.

"I don't know what you mean, Sir," replied Quicks. But the look on his face told another story, and he did nothing to hide it.

"It wasn't you?" Matthys asked Craven, who looked insulted by the assumption he was the culprit. And yet Ferreira shrugged in response, as they both knew he would have taken them if he thought he could get away with it.

"And the sheep?"

"The boys ate well whilst you were away, Sir," replied Quicks.

"That's the truth," added Nooth as he sat down beside the former pickpocket, having bonded over their love of roasted meat.

Craven began to chuckle before bursting out into laughter. The others joined in before making their way back to their own fire.

"I don't understand, Sir. We risked our lives for a pig that was taken away from us because of those turkeys, and you laugh about it?" Paget asked.

"No, we lost our pig because of a pig of an officer."

"But his animals were stolen, were they not?"

"As a soldier you should take what you can get and protect it well."

Paget didn't understand the concept at all, and yet he thought back to the rifle that had been taken from him. He had been accustomed to buying whatever he wished for or asking his father to send to him, but now he was entirely self-dependant he was getting his first insight into how the rest of them lived.

"Yes, Sir, I think I will have to remember that."

A cry of pain and panic rang out before a single shot was let off. Craven ripped his sword from his belt, having left his pistol with his blankets. He rushed towards the sight of the cries as many others rushed on beside him. They could hear Matthys' voice roar as he called others to protect them on all sides, expecting an ambush.

"What is it, Sir?" Paget ran on after the Captain.

As they drew nearer to the scuffle, they heard the growls of wild animals as a man cried out for help. It was one of Ferreira's riflemen, on the ground and being mauled by a wolf. Four more circled about looking to join the fight. The stricken man drew out his sword bayonet and ran it through his attacker. He drew out the bloody blade and waved it about to deter the others as he fought for his life. Rifle fire erupted as their comrades shot at the animals, and they soon fled, not willing to stand for such a fight. Ferreira dropped down beside the man and helped him to his feet, so that he might be able to go on fighting if they needed to, but the battle was over. He looked down at the man's wounds. He was mauled but there were no gushing wounds.

"Is he okay?" Craven asked.

"He will be."

"Damned wolves. I hear they plague our men up and down the country," seethed Paget.

"Because we are the competition. They need food, and we and the French have taken it from them. We've scorched the land and taken everything."

"But they are wild beasts," protested Paget.

"So are we," smiled Craven.

They marched on at first light, all eager to stretch their cold bones. Craven did not even check a map as he merely marched on in search of the enemy.

"Do you think we will find the French soon?" Paget asked Matthys as they went on.

"It can't be long now. Three hundred soldiers on the march cannot go unnoticed for long."

"I do hope so, for I fear if we march for too long, we will find the entire French army." Paget sounded worried.

"Be careful what you wish for." Matthys then pointed off to their flank where French cavalrymen could be seen between a line of trees running almost in parallel with them, but on a path that would intersect ahead of them.

"Scouts?" Paget asked.

"They surely are," replied Craven.

They marched on with anticipation before Craven yelled his orders for them to form up ready to give a volley. Although there was no sign of the French, and so he went forward to investigate with just a few men in a skirmish line. They reach the fork in the road, but there was still no sign of the cavalry. Craven shook his head in disappointment as he returned to the lines.

"They must have seen we were too many for them," he declared and gestured for them to go on.

"I don't like this," whispered Paget.

"Indeed. Now the enemy know where we are and in what strength," replied Matthys wearily.

They went on until finally reaching a stream, at which point Craven drew them to a halt so they might fill their canteens.

"Where are the damn Frenchies now?" Nooth joked.

But nobody replied as they kept a keen eye in every direction for any sign of them. Craven paced up beside Matthys and gestured for Ferreira to join him. He could see a glimmer of movement on the horizon but did not overreact nor draw others to the sight.

"What is it?"

"The cavalry, they won't risk everything against such a

force."

"What are you thinking?"

"You want to bait them?" Matthys joined in the conversation.

Craven nodded in agreement.

"Take thirty of the best shooters we have up there and cover me," he replied to Ferreira as he looked to a ridge to the North.

Ferreira rushed off to do as asked.

"You sure about this?" Matthys asked.

"They wanted to face the enemy, let them," he replied with a smile.

"Nooth, Quicks, on me, and bring ten more men with you!"

Paget quickly selected who he wanted and led them forward to join the Captain, despite not being requested. Craven did not protest as the Lieutenant seemed to bring him luck.

"Stay here, be ready for anything, but do not scare them off," declared Craven.

"Be careful," insisted Matthys.

"Never." Craven went on with the thirteen other men. He led them along a smaller track, and it was not long before they were out of sight of Matthys and the rest of the troops.

"What are we doing out here? It's damned dangerous to be out here so far from the others," declared Nooth.

"Are you scared?"

"Just concerned," he replied sternly.

"The Captain invites the enemy," declared Quicks.

"You do?" Nooth asked.

Craven smiled.

"But why? We have the superior numbers, and we have the advantage."

"We are hooking a fish," replied Quicks.

Nooth looked stunned.

"Do you know why we always robbed the audience at the spectacles your militia out on?"

Nooth shook his head, having no clue.

"Because you brought them to us. Why chase rich people, when you know when and where they'll be."

"Quiet now," insisted Craven. He turned fully around, clocking Ferreira's position on the high ground without stopping to draw attention to them.

"Those brown jackets sure work some wonders, especially at this time of year," admitted Craven.

"Do you want to see us run and collapse in fear? Are you trying to scare us?"

Nooth could see Craven was testing them.

"This is what life is if you fight with us. You are not ready, no matter how much you believe you are."

A French cavalryman appeared on the ridge ahead of them, and then many more, all drawing their swords in readiness to charge.

"Form up!" Craven roared as the thin red line formed beside him in a single rank.

"Make ready!"

Their weapons were brought to full cock. As he looked back to Ferreira's position, he heard the French cavalry officer ahead of them giving his orders as they began their advance. He was smiling as he spotted the Portuguese Captain, but his smile vanished when he noticed several bushes rustling to the flank of

Ferreira's position. A line of French soldiers rose up from cover and opened fire. Ferreira and his riflemen turned to defend themselves as Craven looked back to his modest force and the French cavalry approaching. He realised how much trouble he was in as more than thirty cavalrymen came barrelling towards them. The thundering of their hooves was a horrifying sensation which caused all their pulses to race as they had already reached the charge.

"Present!" Craven ordered. He watched as they took aim, but he kept his own pistol in reserve for when the fighting got closer, and Paget followed his example, "Fire!"

It was a modest volley of twelve rifles. Several of the cavalrymen were thrown from their horses, but it was not nearly enough to deter the charging Frenchmen.

Nooth hurried to reload but Craven pushed him aside. "Get into cover!"

The redcoats scattered as some climbed an embankment, and others, including Craven rushed in amongst some trees and maze-like thick bushes. Craven drew out his sword as he ducked down into some foliage and awaited the cavalry, their charge having been broken by the need to hunt for the scattered troops amongst the difficult terrain.

The Captain looked around and realised he was now all alone. Each man had sought any cover he could, and some of the dense bracken and bushes were taller than a horseman. He could hear the heavy hooves of the cavalrymen as they made their search. He knew if they could delay long enough Matthys would come to the rescue, along with the hundreds of troops they had left further down the road. But he heard the clash of steel and a cry in pain as a man was struck. He could not hide any longer and rushed out search for his comrades and the enemy.

He soon spotted a cavalryman and shot him from the saddle before repeating the same to a second one. It was the best shooting he'd ever made, and yet there was no one there to witness it, not that it was a major feat. The Frenchmen were almost within sword reach when he had shot them, but he would be sure to omit that fact when he bragged about his shooting if they got out alive.

A redcoat soldier came tumbling into view, the furniture of his rifle cut where he had placed it before him in defence, but the weight of the sword blow had thrown him off his feet. For the stroke of a rider was hugely amplified when combined with the weight of the horse, as much a weapon of the cavalryman as the sword was. Craven rushed to the man's aid and pulled him to his feet. They backed away in readiness of fighting the cavalryman together.

"What are you waiting for, hit him!" Craven shouted.

The soldier thrust towards the rider on his bridle arm side which caused the Frenchman to bring his sword over to that side. An awkward task, for a cavalryman must both protect his horse as well as himself, but also work around the animal's head and neck. It was at times difficult and clumsy, and Craven was relying on it, for he had placed himself on the other side of the Frenchman. As the bayonet was parried, he leapt in to take his shot. He thrust his sword into the man's chest, but in the movement of the ride, the blade pierced his thick woollen jacket without doing any damage and for a moment it became stuck. The Frenchman did not whirl his sword around for a strike but merely brought the pommel of the weapon down onto Craven's head. His hat flew from his head as the heavy brass pommel crashed into his skull. Craven's knees buckled and he fell down, losing grip of his sword which was still trapped in the dragoon's coat.

The Captain knew how much danger he was in and desperately tried to get back to his feet, but he was stunned by the blow as blood streamed down his face. He watched the cavalryman grab hold of the muzzle of the musket of the other man and hack down with a cut onto his head that dropped him in one. Craven forced himself upright but wobbled a little. He drew out his dirk with his right hand and took his pistol in his left, which he held by the muzzle as to use it to parry any blows as best he could. It was a horrible improvisation, and he knew he was in serious trouble.

The Frenchman approached and pulled the Andrea Ferrara blade from his jacket. He tossed it away as he held his sabre cocked above his head, priming a blow which would surely be too powerful for the Captain to defend with the modest tools he had left at his disposal. He held them up ready to put up a fight no matter what. The cavalryman rode towards him with a powerful stride like Goliath advancing upon David.

Craven lifted both of his weapons to defend and stop the sabre, but the Frenchman's sabre bounced from his pistol and cut his exposed hand. It was not a deep wound, but the blade ran a long cut across the back of his hand. He winced and dropped the pistol despite his best efforts to keep hold of it. The Frenchman did not relent as he enthusiastically cut down again. Craven held his dirk up to parry. It was a robust dagger, but not nearly enough to withstand the heavy cut of a dragoon's sabre made with full intent and range of motion. Craven's trusty dirk blade was sheared in two and he was left holding just the grip. Little more than an inch of the blade remained where it had separated at the scarf weld where the steel blade was joined to the iron tang. He staggered back, still in a daze and barely able to think let alone to fight.

The Frenchman closed in on him slowly as a predator savouring the kill. Craven was determined to fight on, but he knew the odds were stacked against him in an almost unsurmountable manner. The Frenchman had a wicked grin on his face, but it was soon removed by the crack of a rifle shot. A ball pierced his chest from back to front, and he slumped down dead in the saddle before his horse fled with the body of the soldier bouncing back and forth. Through the cloud of powder smoke came Nooth who rushed up beside the Captain and helped support him.

"Are you okay, Sir?"

Craven looked stunned to see him.

"You didn't think we were ready; do you believe me now?" Nooth jabbed.

Craven smiled and nodded in agreement. He was starting to get his senses back and looked at the remnants of his dirk with disappointment before stuffing the remains into his belt.

"Here." Nooth picked up Craven's pistol, only to find the Captain fumbling about in a bush nearby before returning with his sword which he had found and retrieved.

"Sometimes I think you value that sword more than your life." Nooth passed him the double-barrelled pistol. Craven stuffed it into his sash before holding up the sword to admire it once again.

"When you find a blade like this, you never let it go, for it will be with you until the day you die."

"That isn't much of a claim, considering how close you just came to death, Sir."

"Nonsense, how can they kill me when I have men like you by my side?"

They were the kindest and most welcome words Nooth could expect to hear from his commanding officer and had almost given up hope of ever hearing them.

"You're all right, Nooth," added Craven.

They heard a sporadic volley followed by the roar of many voices. The rest of the Salfords stormed onto the scene to drive the French cavalry away. Craven staggered out of the woods to find a trail of French dead and Matthys sprinting down the road before stopping upon catching sight of him. A few more shots rang out, and they looked up. Ferreira and those who had gone to his aid were chasing off their ambushers.

Quicks appeared from the clearing with a captured French cavalry sabre in hand, the blade soaked with blood. The rest of the small party Craven had led soon reappeared, all still on their feet. The troops gathered around to celebrate a minor victory, waiting to listen to what Craven had to say.

"I was wrong. These boys can fight!"

Cheers rang out as the Salfords celebrated the induction of their newest recruits who had finally seen action against the enemy and proven themselves.

"Next time perhaps a less dangerous test, Sir," replied Paget.

"Never," smiled Craven.

CHAPTER 7

Cheerful conversation echoed out as the soldiers of the Salfords gathered around fires back at their cantonments under the command of Colonel Rooke. Craven marvelled at the sight. They had not been so united and brotherly for as long as he could remember; long before they were forced to depart Lisbon in the face of all the woes caused by Timmerman and in the wake of Hawkshaw's transgressions that had caused it all.

"It was worth it, wasn't it, Sir?" Paget asked.

"Worth what?" Craven asked without looking away from the jubilant scenes.

"Marching out to fight the French and the battle we fought with them."

Craven nodded in agreement.

"For once I agree," admitted Matthys as he joined them.

"Really?" Craven was astonished at his remark.

"They needed it. The new boys needed to be bested, and

the old warhorses needed to know they could place their trust in them. To many it would seem a reckless and dangerous endeavour, but this is war, and everything is dangerous."

Craven looked most pleased with himself.

"And that hand of yours? And your head, Sir?"

"The hand could have been a lot worse and will heal just fine, but that pommel to the head looks like you've been kicked by a horse. I'm amazed you stayed on your feet," added Matthys.

"I've had worse," replied Craven protectively.

But the truth was he had not recovered from the blow and often found his mind wandering distantly at inconvenient moments.

"A hit like that can take months or years to fully recover," said Matthys.

"We do not have years, but a few months until the spring. That's more than enough time."

Matthys looked concerned, and yet he knew there was nothing more he could do, for Craven would not be swayed.

"Are you really okay, Sir?" Paget pressed him.

"I am as good as I can be, and that is all any of us can ever hope for."

They all knew he was far from a good state, but there was nothing more to say or do.

"Captain Craven!" an authoritative voice called out.

Craven turned as if to defend himself to see Major Spring step out from the shadows.

"Colonel Rooke is not happy, Captain."

"I doubt that sour bastard ever is."

Spring struggled to contain a chortle, knowing he should not take pleasure in criticism of a fellow officer, and yet it was hard to not agree and see the funny side.

"The Colonel is most unhappy with you, Captain."

"Well? What is he going to do about it?"

"For now? Nothing. You got him his rifles and powder back. To drag your name through the mud he would have to admit he lost those supplies in the first place, and so drag his own name along behind you."

"We did what he asked, and it cost him nothing. He got what he wanted."

"That is indeed the way the army operates, Captain. We follow orders."

"If that were true, I would not still be here," smirked Craven.

"Yes, well that much is true, I agree."

"So, what punishment do you bring?"

"Punishment? I do not do Colonel Rooke's bidding, Captain. If he still has issue with you, then he must deal with you himself. He had a problem, and I sent him a problem solver. As far as I am concerned, the matter is closed," replied Spring angrily.

Craven appreciated both the logic and the sentiment, but then became suspicious and curious as to the reason for the Major's appearance.

"What do you want, Major?" he groaned.

"Want?" Spring asked incredulously.

"You didn't come here for the conversation."

Spring looked across to Paget, Ferreira, and Hawkshaw who had gathered around him and could see they shared the same suspicion, and so he smiled and shrugged as if to accept that the game was up.

"Spit it out, Major."

"You have orders to ride to Freineda, but you will leave your regiment here where they will continue their training."

Craven frowned in frustration.

"Under that arse Colonel Rooke?"

"I will ensure your men are left to train how they see fit. Captain Hawkshaw will remain to oversee it. The Colonel will not interfere, you have my word," promised Spring.

"And Rooke? Do I have his word?"

"Mine will have to be enough."

Craven groaned in agreement as he was in no position to argue.

"Am I allowed to know the purpose of the journey?"

"You have your orders, Captain. That is the purpose. Good evening, gentlemen," replied Spring mysteriously as he disappeared into the night one more.

"Freineda?" Ferreira asked.

"They say it is Wellington's headquarters," Paget piped up enthusiastically.

"I suppose you would want to come with me, then?"

"Why yes, Sir!" he replied excitedly.

But Craven was not just doing it for him, as he knew the Lieutenant had influence, and even his name would carry them far. It was a tactical decision, and all but Paget could see it.

"It must be of great importance if the General must speak with you personally," added Matthys curiously.

"You will come, too, for I need a voice of reason, especially as this will be a mission of words and not blows."

"And the training?"

Craven nodded in agreement and looked out to those still

celebrating their successes, reliving the skirmish as fondly as those who had fought at Talavera and Albuera.

"They have all been through it now. Your training saw them through, and Hawkshaw is more than capable of keeping them going."

"We should bring several more capable men, for the road can still be treacherous." replied Matthys.

"Charlie, Moxy, and Ellis." He studied the group, "And him." Craven looked across to Amyn.

Matthys looked surprised.

"That man survived an ambush which killed hundreds, not a bad ally to have around."

"I'd remind you that whilst he survived, none of those beside him did."

Craven chuckled.

"He's coming. He has the eyes of a hawk, and I would have those eyes whilst we travel with so few." And yet Craven was surprised to see Matthys did not approve, "What is it that you dislike about him?"

"He is no Christian."

"Neither am I," snapped Craven.

Matthys shrugged as if he didn't like that either.

"I'd be careful who you say that around, Sir. Many a man has been killed for his lack of faith," replied Paget.

"Any man is welcome to come and test mine. For my faith is in tempered steel of the finest quality," he smiled.

It was hard to disagree with that.

"We ride in the morning."

"At first light, Sir?"

"By God no," protested Craven, "First night back in a real

bed and you would have us dragged from it at the first chance?"

Paget looked most put out, but Matthys smiled.

"Enjoy yourself, Lieutenant, for tomorrow there is work to be done," declared Craven.

"It is hardly work when one loves what he does," replied Paget.

"Bring me more wine!" Craven roared, eliciting a great cheer from the troops.

* * *

Paget ran a grooming brush across his beloved horse Augustus. The sun had been up for more than an hour, and he must have been at it since at least then as the animal was the smartest in all the army and a far cry from many of the sorry-looking overworked animals seen on campaign.

"I've never seen a man so in love with his horse," smiled Charlie as she saw to her own mount.

"A good horse can be the difference between success and failure, between life and death. How a man looks after an animal speaks volumes about his character," declared Paget proudly.

Charlie smiled. She had meant to toy with him, and yet his response was endearing. He would not be shamed for his care and love of his horse, and that made her love him more, but also dwell on how true his words were.

"Is everything okay?" Paget asked in concern to see her pained expression.

"I was just thinking how different life could have been if I'd possessed a horse when I most needed one."

"On the retreat to Corunna?" asked Paget, knowing that is where her mind had gone, for that horrific experience plagued her continually. She nodded in agreement.

"I am not sure a horse would have survived the ordeal. I dread to think of having to take Augustus through such a hellish experience."

"Hell? That would have been better, at least it would have been warm," she replied, trying to make light of the memory despite the sadness in her eyes.

"I pray you never have to endure such a time ever again," he replied sincerely.

"Death would be better," she admitted.

It was hard for Paget to imagine how horrific an experience it must have been. Few of those who had lived through it ever spoke of the details, which only made him imagine the worst. He knew he could not picture an experience worse than the reality of what they went through.

"It still surprises me when I remember that the Captain went through it, too."

"It was Craven who got me through it. For without him I would never have made it. I owe him my life, and I will never forget it."

Paget was in awe of what that must mean. For they had all held one another's lives in their hands, and yet that experience three years previously was the one which stood out above all others by a mile. He did not press any further because the wounds were still evidently very raw.

"What do you think Lord Wellington wants with the Captain?"

"Craven is a weapon, so I imagine Old Nosey intends to

point him in his direction."

Paget laughed. "Could he not have sent orders along with Major Spring for that purpose?" Paget thought about it further.

"Then I imagine it will be some great big secret as to how he wants to direct Craven, as much as you steer a battering ram."

"Yes, I imagine so," pondered Paget.

The door to their stable was thrown open, causing a gust of cold air to waft through. Craven stepped in, looking remarkably fresh considering his well-earned reputation.

"I thought you meant to sleep the morning through, Sir?"

"No, I just didn't want to be woken."

"Was there not enough wine last night?" Charlie asked with no tact at all, implying he would not have risen so early had it been for the shortage.

"There never is," smiled Craven.

They were soon on their way, and as they got out into the open country it suddenly dawned on Paget just how few they were. He peered around with suspicion and began to feel awfully vulnerable.

"What worries you, Mr Paget?"

"Sir, we marched out into similar land with three hundred men and still got into trouble. Now we are just a handful."

"The road to Freineda is a busy one with British troops travelling up and down regularly. You will not find a Frenchman within ten miles of the route," replied Matthys as he tried to calm Paget's nerves.

Yet Paget would not settle until they went over a ridge and finally could see they were not alone. Wagons and troops made their way back and forth on the route.

"You worry too much, Lieutenant," declared Craven.

"Perhaps I do not worry enough? For there would be no surprises if we all kept a keen eye on all things," he retorted.

"The Lieutenant has a point," declared Matthys.

"Yes, he does, and that's what makes him so annoying."

Charlie nodded along in agreement. She reached across and punched Paget gently on the arm in a friendly fashion, something she would never do in sight of an officer outside of the Salfords, for it would be considered assault. Paget grumbled as he looked away, but in truth he didn't mind it. Being told he was overzealous was nothing short of a compliment in his eyes.

"How far is this place?" Moxy asked.

"We'll be there by nightfall," replied Craven.

"Good, we can sleep under a roof again and might even have the luxury of a bed!" Moxy roared gleefully.

"I wouldn't count on it. Freineda is a miserable little village with little to offer. I heard one officer describe the accommodations of every kind as wretched as it is possible to conceive," replied Matthys.

"Charming," replied Moxy.

"Why then would Lord Wellington slum it in such an awful place?" Paget asked.

"Because it is only fifteen miles from the Spanish border fortress of Ciudad Rodrigo."

Matthys looked at the Captain in disbelief.

"You think I don't follow these things?"

"I did have my doubts."

"You think Lord Wellington means to pass into Spain and besiege the fortress?" Paget asked excitedly.

"Of course, I do, and the whole army knows it. We just don't know when."

"How can you be so sure, Sir?"

"Because it is one of the keys to Spain, that and Badajoz. Wellington cannot go into Spain without first taking those two city fortresses which block our way."

"March, then?"

"Or February, perhaps," replied Matthys.

Paget sighed. "It feels so far away."

"The time will come soon enough, and then you will wish it hadn't," replied Matthys.

"Why would you say that?"

"Assaulting a heavily guarded fortress is nasty business."

"But with great risks comes great rewards. A man may be rewarded with instant promotions at a battle like that."

"And many more will be rewarded with death," grimaced Matthys.

"But it is a great honour to be first through the breach upon an assault, is it not?" Paget responded with great enthusiasm.

"Is honour worth more than your life?" Craven asked.

"Why yes, Sir. For we all must die, but to do so honourably is a choice that every man must make," he declared proudly.

Charlie looked upon him in deep concern. "You still believe in all of that?"

"How could I not?"

"My husband was taken from me. He was an honourable man, but there was no honour in his death," she cried.

Paget was silent. It was the most that she had ever shared about her old life in all the time he had known her. Out of respect, he said nothing more on the matter.

"Promise me if you are ever there at the scene of such an

assault, you will never volunteer to lead it?"

"I…I cannot make that promise," he stuttered, unable to compromise the morals he so strongly defended.

"Don't worry, a Salfords man will never be given that supposed honour. Every regiment in the army is filled with richer and stupider fools who would lead the way and use their influence to climb all the way to their own deaths," replied Matthys.

"But someone must go first, must they not?"

"Yes, but there is no need to go so eagerly to your death."

"If someone must do it, better it be a man who will do it proudly than a coward."

"No man who stormed a breach can ever be called a coward, not in all of his days," replied Craven sternly.

"Might a man do a brave thing when following orders but still be a coward, Sir?"

Craven shook his head.

"A coward would refuse and die before a firing squad before that."

Paget was stunned as if he could not understand it, but he was silent the rest of the journey and spent many hours in a haze, dwelling on it all in his own mind. The discussion left the mood of the group soured and few spoke at all for the rest of the way. They passed many supply wagons, messengers, and other troops until finally they reached the sign for Freineda.

It was indeed a tiny little village situated in the middle of a barren plain. It had nothing to offer anyone but the locals who worked the land and called it home. Aside from the flutter of candle lights, more so than would be expected of a village, and the guards on duty, there was little to give away the new inhabitants. There was no great tented cantonment on the leadup to the town and only those billeted in the village houses could be residing there. There was certainly nothing to suggest it was the headquarters of Wellington himself.

"I am surprised Sir Arthur would stoop to such lows," said Paget as he got a good look himself.

"I imagine he does for the same reason he is seen galloping about the battlefield."

"Why is that, Sir?"

"Because to the General location is everything."

They rode on into the narrow streets of white walled buildings. It was a dreary place. There was not a structure more than two storeys tall, and they soon found the General's headquarters. It was unmistakable, for it was the largest house in the village, which was not saying much. It made Colonel Rooke's quarters look positively palatial. Across the small village square was the local church. Several officers gazed upon Craven and his comrades with suspicion, and they were right to do so, as they appeared entirely out of place.

"Can I help you?" asked one of them.

"Captain James Craven, I have orders to report to Wellington."

Another officer came out from a nearby doorway, a heavy cavalry officer.

"Captain Craven! You were indeed sent orders to report here, but not to Wellington."

The first man to have questioned him turned his nose up and walked away, almost disappointed that he was in the right place after all. Craven looked even more surprised, as now he had no clue as to what they were doing there. They watched the coming and goings of Wellington's headquarters as if expecting to be called in at any moment.

"You may take your horses to the stable situated down that road. They will be expecting you, but you must move the animals at first light, for it is a little tight here," said the officer politely.

"Who am I reporting to?"

"It is not for me to say, but please be prompt, and I will see you on your way."

Craven frowned before leading them on.

"Is this anything to do with Colonel Rooke?"

"I am afraid I do not know of such an officer."

He gave up asking questions and did as was requested.

"I thought we came to see the General, Sir?" Paget asked.

"Major Spring never said as such," replied Ellis rather astutely.

"Yes, we made our own assumptions, and let that be a lesson to us all," added Matthys.

They saw to their horses before returning to the dragoon officer who had been polite to them but never given his name.

"Follow me. Your men may wait in the hall," he said as he led him inside.

It seemed to be the second largest house in the village, and so Craven knew someone of importance must have taken up residence, and yet he did not have the slightest clue as to who it could be.

"Captain James Craven of the Salford Rifles, Sir," introduced the officer. He showed Craven into a space which had been hastily converted into the personal office of whoever had summoned him. He stepped inside to see a striking figure he recognised instantly, but only from paintings of the man. Standing upright in the candlelight behind a table was slight man in his forties with an astute and confident demeanour. His gaze could cut a hole through many a man. It was Gaspard Le Marchant, now Major General and commander of a heavy cavalry brigade. He needed no introduction as Craven was intimately familiar with his history.

Le Marchant had been a cavalryman since the war in the low countries in the early part of the 1790s. He had been so struck by his experiences of soldiers and soldiering that upon his return he championed such major reforms there was not a man in the Army who did not know his name. Le Marchant had been disappointed by both the swords and swordsmanship of the army he had served in those early years. He had then worked with the renown cutler Henry Osborn to create a new sword for the cavalry. A shorter and sturdier weapon which was handier and delivered brutal cleaving blows, the now famous symbol of the light cavalry; the stirrup hilted and broad deeply curved sabre which had carried the British through a great many battles over many years. Le Marchant was a symbol of British swordsmanship and a hero to any man who trained in the methods of cut and thrust fighting. Craven was stunned to meet a man who was more a mythical figure to those who followed the way of the blade.

"Captain Craven, what a pleasure it is to meet you."

CHAPTER 8

"My name is Gaspard, General Gaspard Le Marchant."

"I...I know who you are, Sir," replied Craven with the same stutter and hesitation that Paget often suffered from when he was an equal mix of anxious and excited.

"Welcome, Captain."

"Thank you, Sir."

And yet he found his gaze wandering as it was attracted to the glimmering reflection of candlelight from the steel scabbard of the General's sword hanging from a hat stand. Le Marchant smiled as he noticed Craven fixate on the weapon.

"You have quite the reputation as a swordsman," declared Le Marchant.

"As do you, Sir." He remained entirely fixated on the sabre as the General took it from the stand.

"I designed this sword, you know."

"I am well aware, Sir."

The sabre was incongruous beside the General's heavy cavalry uniform and wide bicorne, a uniform which looked so antiquated in the British Army today. Le Marchant had made his fame as a light cavalryman, and yet here he was in charge of a heavy cavalry brigade. He had not adopted their sword, instead keeping the one he so lovingly developed. By regulation he should wear the large straight sword of the heavies, and yet a high-ranking officer could largely do whatever they pleased. In truth, Le Marchant had spent as many years with the heavy cavalry as the light, if not more, but he would forever be associated with the latter for having created the sword they now used to devastating effect.

"This sword was gifted to be by Henry Osborn upon the acceptance of the pattern by the King," he declared as he passed it to Craven, "The whole of the bloody cavalry should have had 'em, ah, I did what I could. Here."

Craven's eyes lit up as he took the sword. It was a common weapon which he had been around for what felt like all his life, having been in service for fifteen years now.

"So, this is where it all began?" he asked as he took the sword and admired it.

The sword was of the standard pattern for officers, which was functionally no different to that used by the troopers, with only a few small cosmetic improvements such as wire wrap over the leather grip, but as Craven drew the blade the blue and gilt was revealed as it gleamed in the candlelight. The sword felt nimble in Craven's hands, despite the formidable cutting power it possessed. As he moved it back and forth, he could tell it was an incredibly fine example. Many officers opted for lighter and more refined swords than their troopers, but Le Marchant's sword was of full trooper's weight. Yet somehow it felt more agile, which is when Craven realised it was shorter than standard; shorter even than his infantry officer's sword by a good inch, which was extreme when almost every cavalryman in every army carried very long blades. Le Marchant had an even shorter example of an already very short pattern of weapon for its type.

"It's short."

"Just how I wanted it, but we rarely get exactly what we want in the army, do we?" he smiled.

Craven continued to marvel at the blade as Le Marchant went on, as if glad to finally have someone as passionate about swords as him with which to discuss the finer points.

"Without a doubt, the expertly used scimitar blades of the Turks, Mamelukes, Moors, and Hungarians have proved that a light sword, if equally applicable to a cut or thrust, is preferable to any other."

"I count a Mameluke amongst my men, Sir, and I am certain that he would agree, for he is a most formidable swordsman."

"The way you look at that sabre it surprises me to not see one on your side, and that you only carry the infantryman's sword, a modest weapon for such a famous fencer to use."

It was true that before it was drawn, his sword looked particularly unremarkable. If anything, it would be considered scruffy, for so much of the gold gilt decoration was missing. But Craven drew his beloved sword and marvelled at it with the same eyes he gave the Le Marchant's sabre in his left, before passing it to the General.

"Andrea Ferrara?" Le Marchant marvelled at it.

"Yes, Sir."

"How can a poor Captain afford such a treasure?"

"By not paying for it," replied Craven with a smile.

Le Marchant did not press further but was fascinated by it.

"I see you are taken by my sabre, and yet you choose a very different weapon for yourself. You need not carry a sword which meets the regulations of a line infantry officer. Frankly, I think you could use whatever you like, for you are certainly not known for living by the rules."

"Your sabre favours the power of the cut, and I imagine that is quite useful to the men of the light cavalry."

"And you? What must you look for in a sword, Captain?" Le Marchant asked with genuine curiosity.

"Celerity, for what good is a powerful cutting sword if you are beaten to the mark by a lighter one."

"And when that light sword must parry the heavy one?"

"Any blow can be parried by a light sword if done correctly, even a smallsword may parry your cavalry sabre."

"But there is that caveat, done correctly. Soldiers may be taught to do something perfectly, but will they then do it at the right moment? The army would have our men use the point more like the French, but in the heat of battle an Englishman always swings like the axeman, and I would embrace that natural instinct and make every one of them the most formidable axeman as they can be."

Craven smiled and nodded at the prospect.

"Ah, look at me, going on and on once more. It is good to have a fellow scholar of the sword with which to make my arguments. I have wanted to make your acquaintance for some time, Captain."

"You have?"

"A man who has made a name for himself with his sword, how could I not?" smiled Le Marchant, "Will you join me in a drink?"

"How could I refuse?"

They put both swords away, and the General gestured for him to sit down. He poured out two large measures and slid one across the table. Craven took it up and marvelled at the quality of the receptacle. It was fit for a lord, and the alluring smell of a high-quality Madeira wafted across his nose.

"To damn fine swords, and the silly fools who wield them," declared Le Marchant as they toasted and drank. Craven sighed in relief. He had expected a very different welcome, and nothing like what the evening had become. As he thought about it further, he became a tad suspicious.

"You didn't just summon me here to talk about swords, did you?"

"If only life were so simple," admitted Le Marchant.

"Well, then, let us get it over with."

"I have to admit, Captain that your existence both insults and amuses me in equal measure. You are everything I have tried so hard to root out of the army. I have devoted my life to a military academy which would increase the education and the training of the officer corps of this army and all which will follow it. And yet here you are, a drunken rogue who has none of that and does as he pleases. What's more, you get away with it, because your results cannot be denied. But you also remind me a little of myself many years ago, and I would be a fool to not respect all you have achieved. We have a very different approach to soldiering, Captain, like our taste in swords, but there is a valuable lesson here; that there are many ways to achieve success, and none of us have all of the answers."

"If you will, Sir, I would very much like a straight answer as to what I am doing here," demanded Craven politely.

"The honest truth is that Lord Wellington asked me to speak to you personally, swordsman to swordsman."

Craven sighed as he was expecting the bad news to drop any second.

"You ruffle many feathers, Captain, and senior officers don't much like their feathers being ruffled by junior officers. It causes a great deal of trouble, you see, from all the way to Wellington and back to London. Wellington wants to make you a Major, and you rightly should be," said Le Marchant.

"That is what I am doing here?"

Le Marchant nodded in agreement as he got up and began to pace, looking quite uncomfortable.

"But it's not what you want?"

"If you had asked me a year ago, I would have said yes, certainly, but now I am hesitant."

"Why, Sir?"

"I told you I have devoted my life to the military college and the education of the officers of the future. A role I was honoured to have held for so many years, but I, too, was promoted. I was promoted out of my position. It was a curse disguised as a blessing, for upon promotion I have become considered too senior to fulfil my former role, and so you find me here."

"You do not wish to lead a cavalry brigade under Wellington?"

"Of course, what cavalry officer would not? But many

men could do what I do here. I could have done so much more as a teacher."

"But you are Gaspard Le Marchant, Sir."

"I am but one man, and what difference can one man make?"

"A great deal I have learned."

Le Marchant smiled as he realised the topic of the conversation had quickly moved on from its intended purpose.

"Become Major Craven. You have earned it, and you need it."

"Is that an order, Sir?"

"I cannot force it upon you."

Craven was deep in thought and looked most uncomfortable with the prospect.

"Listen, Captain, Wellington told me to not take no for an answer, but I think a man such as yourself deserves a fair contest. Come out to our exercises tomorrow afternoon, and we will make a contest of it. If I win, you are Major Craven."

Craven's hesitation quickly slipped away. The gambler in him could not resist as a smile stretched across his face.

"You're on."

Craven sat back in amusement, sipping on his drink as if already celebrated his success.

"Will you join us for dinner? Say you will," insisted Le Marchant.

"Of course. I travel with another officer, a Lieutenant Paget. He may be of humble rank, but he is close friends with the family of Lord Wellington."

"I have heard about this young man, and I am most intrigued to make his acquaintance. Now, I have had some beds prepared for you on the edge of this wretched place. It's not much, but a soldier could do a lot worse."

"Thank you, Sir."

Craven finished his drink and got up without asking to take his leave. Le Marchant looked flustered but also amused by his insolence, but said nothing, despite it being evident he would have scolded any other man for doing what the Captain had done.

"Be back here for eight o'clock, Captain, and we will feast on more than just food, for there are many stories I would have you tell."

"Yes, Sir."

"Major Bishop will show you to your quarters," he declared as the door opened, and the man who had shown him in presented himself.

"You are Bishop?"

"I am, and it's a pleasure to meet you, Captain."

"With this many kind words, I would be right to imagine a trap, for it seems too good to be true."

"Be careful what you wish for, Craven, you might just get it," chortled Le Marchant.

But Craven showed no fear, for he would meet any test of arms with the utmost confidence, and there would be no repeats of his less than satisfactory performance against Nooth. He had long since been pulled out of the drunken despair which had led to those losses. He followed the Major out with so much on his mind, but most of all he was in astonishment to have finally met the great army swordsman that was Gaspard Le Marchant.

"What do you think of the General?" Bishop asked.

"I feel like I have known him for years without ever having

met him."

"He is a good man, and just the sort we need to turn this war around."

"You don't think it's going well?"

"I know that Wellington's victory at Talavera is closing on three years past. That was the last time the British successfully campaigned in Spain. Wellington has held on here against some tremendous odds, but I'd hardly call it progress, would you?"

Craven shrugged and nodded in agreement.

"1812 will be different, will it not?"

"Gaspard will be sure of it, for he will not wait in Portugal. He will be charging on to Madrid just as soon as this wretched winter ends."

"You are close with him, then?" Craven was surprised at both the familiarity and faith he placed in the General.

"I am, but don't for a minute think that clouds my judgement. I follow Gaspard because of what he is as a man, not who he is as a name, rank, or title."

Craven liked that mantra as he believed in it, too. Paget was eager for news as he and the others followed on as Bishop led the way.

"What news, Sir?" pressed the Lieutenant.

"We are to dine tonight with General Le Marchant," replied Craven calmly, pretending to not know how excited that would make the young Lieutenant.

"Truly, Sir?"

"Truly."

"But we are not dressed for the occasion, Sir," complained Paget, ever the dapper and fashion-conscious officer. Craven laughed as he looked at Paget, whose uniform looked barely a few weeks old and in pristine condition to anyone who was not looking at it under a microscope, and a damn sight smarter than his own uniform.

"You'll do just fine," replied Bishop.

They were shown to their lodgings, a dining room in a modest house where a line of simple mattresses and blankets had been laid out across one wall and the furniture moved to the opposite side to create a cramped living space. It was little better than sleeping in a barn, but vastly more comfortable than many of the harsh nights they had spent under canvas, or worse still, the open air.

"I'm afraid I can offer you gentlemen no better accommodation. There are some colonels living in lesser conditions in this place, but Wellington will not retreat to find something better."

"It will do just fine, thank you."

"Then I shall see you later this evening, gentlemen."

"We look forward to it, Sir," replied Paget excitedly.

Craven had a lot to think about as he slumped down onto a chair. Matthys knew the expression well, for it was the look of a troubled mind at a crossroads.

"What is it?"

"Wellington would have me made a major."

The room fell silent for a moment.

"Congratulations, Sir!" Paget finally cried.

But Craven shrugged, and Paget could not understand it.

"What is the matter, Sir?"

"The Captain could have been a major a long time ago if he'd wanted it," declared Matthys.

"Sir?" Paget expected an explanation.

"With promotion comes responsibility, and it's harder to keep your head down," admitted Craven.

"That is how the old Craven would talk," added Charlie.

"It's true. You have that responsibility now, and you no longer hide in the shadows," agreed Matthys.

"You already do the job of a major, Sir. Why not accept the pay and promotion that you deserve?"

Craven looked uncertain.

"What about you? What do you think?" he asked Moxy as the one who usually spoke the most and yet had remained silent.

"If the army wants to give you more money, you should say yes. Why wouldn't you?" replied the Welshman.

"You should do what your heart desires," replied Ellis in an uncharacteristic moment, for he rarely spoke at all without being prompted.

"What would you know about being an officer?" Moxy joked.

"Plenty." They all looked to the reserved and reclusive rifleman, "I used to be one," he replied plainly.

If anyone else had said it they would have laughed at what could only be a blatant lie, and yet somehow, they had no reason to doubt it from a man who was forever dependable. None of them really knew Ellis well nor had ever gotten much insight into his former life, not even Matthys.

"You were?" asked the Sergeant in disbelief.

"I was," he replied calmly.

"What changed?" Paget asked.

"It wasn't the life for me. I don't want to command men. I do not want to socialise at the mess. I wanted a simple life."

Still, nobody had reason to doubt him, and there was a

sense amongst them all that some pieces had fallen into place. He had always been an oddball and an outsider, but few could ever put a finger on why, aside from his aloof nature.

"And yet you follow Craven?" Charlie laughed.

"I said simple, not easy."

Laughter rang out about the room. It was the first time any of them had ever heard Ellis utter a word in humour. But as the noise died down, it got Craven thinking.

"Is that true?"

"When have I ever told you something that is not?" he replied stoically.

"Follow my heart, you say?"

"Do what you want to do."

Craven appreciated the sentiment, but it left him no better equipped to make the decision. The time passed quickly, and Paget was soon adjusting his uniform to look his best for dinner, cursing under his breath that he had not been given the time and resources to be at his best. As opposed to Craven who merely sat deep in contemplation, ready to meet the General in the same manner as he had arrived in town.

"Sir, you know we go to dine with a general?"

"First and foremost, he is a cavalryman, not some rich buffoon with more money than sense." But he soon laughed at his own assessment, "Well, Le Marchant certainly has the money, but he has the sense as well. I was born into the wrong family," he smiled.

The door to their room opened, and several locals came in carrying trays of food and drink, resulting in a great cheer from Moxy and Charlie. Major Bishop was with them, now dressed in all his finery for the meal.

"When some of the families of this little village heard that Captain Craven was amongst them, they insisted on bringing a feast for you and your companions."

Craven shot to his feet and humbly accepted the gifts. It was a mighty gift indeed, for he knew how sparse food could be in these days.

"Please extend my gratitude, but this is too much," he replied to Bishop.

Moxy looked aghast that they might miss out on the mighty feast which was before them.

"Take the gift, Captain, for it would be rude not to. You have risked your life for their country and their countrymen. You all have, and they know it. Let them thank you in the one way they can."

"Thank you, thank you," insisted Craven, but the locals shrugged off his gratitude as if it were unnecessary.

"It is time to be on your way, Captain. I am sure your men will eagerly devour these gifts."

Moxy and Charlie looked upon the platters of food like starving wolves, almost salivating at the mere sight of it.

Craven sighed, knowing he was going to another grilling as those around him insisted on promotion. He looked to Ellis who nodded back, having imparted all that he needed to, and Craven was grateful for it. His destiny now remained in his own hands. He picked up his sword belt and hooked it about his body but left his pistol and sorry-looking broken dirk on a table. He and Paget then followed the Major.

"Have you ever met the General?" Craven asked Paget.

"No, Sir, our paths have never crossed, and yet it seems as though they should have. But even if they had, I would have been nothing but a fresh young officer, and what time would a General have given me?"

"I think you might have been pleasantly surprised. Gaspard is most devoted to the next generation of young officers," replied Bishop.

"And now you get to meet the General as a famous veteran of many battles," added Craven.

"Famous, Sir?"

"The General knew your name and was eager to meet you. What else would you call that?"

Paget beamed with joy at the prospect. They were led back into the place where Craven had first met Le Marchant and into a cosy dining room with many candles lit. The General was waiting them with several staff to cater to their meal beside a warming fireplace, but only enough seating for the four of them. Craven and Paget had expected something rather more grandiose.

"Evening, gentlemen."

Paget snapped to attention, but Craven casually took a seat.

"Lieutenant Berkeley Paget, Salford Rifles, Sir."

"I know who you are, my dear Lieutenant. Craven talks as if he knows me for having read about my exploits, but I have to tell you I think I rather know the two of you fine gentlemen rather better for the same reason."

"You do, Sir?" queried Paget as if a prank was being played on him.

"Take a seat," insisted Le Marchant with a smile.

Wine was soon poured and passed around rather casually.

"To success in Spain," toasted Le Marchant.

They all repeated the toast and sipped on the wine which was fine indeed.

"Careful on that stuff, Craven, for you will want to be on top form tomorrow," advised the General.

"Do tell, Sir, for what I beg you tell me," Paget said to Craven.

"The General and I have a wager to settle."

"Not with live blades?" Paget gasped.

"No, nothing like that, Lieutenant, all in good spirits."

"Then I eagerly await the experience, but I must warn you, Sir, Captain Craven is a very formidable swordsman."

"As is the General," admitted Craven.

Steaming hot food was placed before them, and all four men were quick to dig in.

"Meaning no insult, Sir, but I would have expected more men at your table."

"Sometimes, but not tonight, for I would give my full attention to the men of the Salfords this night."

"And your wife, Sir? She does not travel with you?"

Gaspard hesitated for a moment. His face turned to stone, but he quickly recovered, even though Major Bishop did not.

"I am afraid my good wife passed away soon after we departed England only this summer. Died in childbirth, you see."

"I am so sorry, Sir. I did not mean…" gushed Paget in the deepest apology and sympathy.

"No, no, it is a kind thing for you to ask after my wife when so many others would not have," replied Le Marchant.

"My sympathies," added Craven.

"Death is all a matter of life for men like you."

"It is the deaths we least expect which strike the hardest," replied Craven.

Gaspard was close to loosing off a tear as he nodded in agreement.

"I thank you for that." He held up his glass, "Let us toast then to my late wife, the Lady Mary, the best a man could ever hope to find."

"To Lady Mary," they replied, holding up their glasses in a brief moment of silence out of respect, Le Marchant sat back and smiled as the melancholy passed.

"You are not the man I expected, Captain," he admitted to Craven.

"A swordsman must never be exactly what you expect, or he has already failed."

"Quite, but I do not speak of your skills with the sword, for we shall see those tomorrow, of which I am most eager to do so. But I imagined you an ill-tempered and prickly sort of fellow, and I should know how to spot one. I have been all my life squabbling and quarrelling, and unable to get out of troubled waters. I have a temper, you see, and I work every day to ensure that no man may accuse me of such manners."

"You will see the best side of me when I am beside a roaring fire, well fed, and with wine in hand."

Le Marchant and Bishop laughed in agreement. Neither man had experienced the harsh realities of the war in Portugal, but they were both old soldiers with plenty of experience under their belts to know the sensation well.

"I will speak plainly, Captain. You are hated amongst the officers of this army, and loved by the men, and so the officers hate you further."

Craven shrugged as if he did not care.

"And this is why you are not the man I expected you to be. A scoundrel, a ruffian, a rogue, this is what I have been told about you. But now I see it is not true at all. You have no respect for authority, but I see you have no shortage of discipline. I can see why many gentlemen would hate you, but if every one of them was a Captain Craven, I imagine we would be having this meal in Madrid."

It was a sore point, for Madrid was the city Wellington had aimed for during the campaign which led to the battle of Talavera. It seemed like a lifetime ago now.

"I can fight well, damn well, but I do not claim to be anything more."

"Maybe that is all you need to be."

"I am not sure you believe that, Sir. You have led the infantry and the cavalry. You have set up a military college and reformed the arms and training of the cavalry. You are no master of one."

"And neither are you, for a single swordsman can win a duel, but not a battle. You have forged a force which is most formidable, and so you are no master of one trade either."

"It is true. The Captain has brought together some of the most unlikely of fellows, and yet what they have achieved under his command is quite amazing," added Paget.

Le Marchant smiled and nodded in agreement, pouring himself some more wine, not waiting for another to do it for him.

"They say you are a ruffian, Captain, but what ruffian could charm the worst thieves and brigands and some of the politest young gentleman to his side at the same time, and bond them together?"

Craven shrugged.

"It could never be done in peacetime, Captain, but out here on the bloody frontier, the normal rules do not all apply, do they?"

"Indeed," admitted Craven.

"I'll be honest with you, Captain, though I am sure nothing of what I am about to say is a surprise, only that it is being admitted to you. The mood amongst the army is very poor indeed, not just amongst the common soldier, but with officers of the most senior rank. A dark cloud hangs over us all, I am afraid. Officers write home to their sweethearts and share these gloomy tidings, some of which have even been shared with the newspapers, much to Wellington's chagrin. The worse of it is they are right. I do not know how long we may maintain this resistance against the might of Napoleon's armies, but whilst we still live and breathe with our feet on Portuguese and Spanish land, I would have us fight with a spirit worthy of the British name."

Paget was dismayed by the news and yet still spurred on by Le Marchant's sentiment.

"We were never winning this war. Not since Corunna. We celebrated survival, not victory. Talavera was no different, nor the Lines of Torres Vedras. We hang on by a thread, but the papers report it all as a great victory," replied Craven.

"Then if we are to lose this war, let us do it in the most British of ways," smiled Le Marchant.

Craven sighed in dismay.

"You see, Captain. You have known the hardships more than most, and yet this melancholy does not curse you like it does so many in the army. This is why Wellington would promote you. If he cannot lift the mood of those around him, he certainly can promote more enthusiastic men into those positions. If only you were a General!" Le Marchant chuckled.

"I see you have changed strategy to get me to accept the promotion?"

"Far from it. Wellington told me to not take no for an answer, but I do not believe in thrusting a soldier into a role he does not truly desire, for he will never give it his all."

"But you would have me to it upon the loss of a wager?"

"Yes, because I know you are a man of your word, which few understand or appreciate, and if you lose to me in a fair fight, you would do the honourable thing and move forward with all enthusiasm."

"But I won't lose," replied Craven confidently.

"Then you have nothing to worry about," snickered Le Marchant.

Craven was most curious about the man before him, for he was like no General he had ever met. He spoke more like a fencing master than a Brigade commander.

"To a fine contest then." Le Marchant held up his glass.

"May the best man win," answered Craven.

CHAPTER 9

Matthys awoke at first light to find Craven was already awake in a most unusual sight. He was sitting at the window deep in thought, and remarkably did not look any worse for wear after his drinks with the General. Matthys went to sit beside him and waited for him to share his woes, but when he did not, the Sergeant pressed him.

"Do you fret over the fight or the promotion?"

"A friendly bout is nothing to fret over, and I will win it anyway."

"What would be so terrible about being Major Craven?"

"I was never born to be a major. I only took a captaincy in Portugal because the pay was half decent and the responsibility low. I was brought here to teach men how to fight, not to lead them."

"And what is it you have been doing these past years?"

"Fighting."

"And the soldiers who have fought with you?"

"I've done what I can to keep them alive and help them win."

"Is that not leading?"

Craven groaned in agreement.

"I won't tell you want to do, but I will tell you this. You deserve this promotion, and it will mean a lot to all of us to see you get it, and you'll gain a lot of autonomy. A major who reports directly to Lord Wellington holds a lot of power."

Craven shrugged. He had always gone and done as he pleased, and yet there were often a great many obstacles placed before him by his superiors, and that fact was hard to argue with.

"Then I should accept it?"

"I think you should follow Ellis' advice and not let others decide for you."

Craven smiled as he shook his head.

"Ellis? An officer. I suppose it makes some sense now to think about it, but it goes to show you can know a man for years and still not really understand him."

"You are only just learning this now?" Matthys joked.

"I'm glad it amuses you." Ellis was awake and had been listening the whole time.

"Why? Why not tell us?"

"Because I didn't want a hundred questions. I just wanted to be left alone."

Craven shrugged and nodded in agreement, for a simple life was an envious one.

"You are full of surprises," admitted Matthys.

"I just thought you were shy and awkward," replied Craven.

"Sometimes what a man doesn't say is as important as what he does."

Now that was a sentiment which resonated with Craven, and he could understand it as a fencer. For what information you give the opponent was just as important as what you withheld, if not more so.

"Do you want to get some practice in?" Matthys asked.

"Do you think I need it?"

"They say Le Marchant is a great swordsman and a supreme rider, too," noted Paget.

"A good swordsman by the army standards, but that is nothing compared to gladiators who have dedicated their lives to using the sword and not soldiering."

"Yes, I imagine so, Sir. It will be a most exciting contest, I am sure."

Craven shrugged as if it didn't mean that much to him, but they all knew that was not true. Any chance to cross blades with a well-known swordsman was a treat for the Captain.

"What shall we do with the morning, Sir?"

"Must we do something?"

Moxy nodded in agreement from where he was still lying in bed looking supremely comfortable, and Craven seemed to agree.

"The whole army has been stuck waiting out this winter, idle and bored, and yet you would choose to do nothing?" Paget asked him.

Moxy shrugged as if he had no excuses for his laziness.

"The army might have been idle, but we have not been," added Craven.

"A little excitement recently, I will admit, but only a few

days of adventure in several months," complained Paget.

"There is a lot to be said for quiet days, and I think you will come to welcome them in a few years' time," smiled Matthys.

But Paget did not look convinced and looked restless for a few minutes before shooting to his feet, causing Craven to smile in amusement that the young man could not sit still for long.

"There is a world out there to experience, and I will go to experience it," he declared as he went for the door.

"I'll go with him." Charlie rushed on after him.

They got out into the fresh cold air as a breeze swept through and carried away the unique musk which an army brought with them everywhere they went.

"I am not sure you will be welcome everywhere we go. Some officers will not appreciate your presence, for we should not even be associating with one another," Paget said with much concern, his head darting back and forth as he looked as passers-by, as if expecting to be caught doing something he shouldn't.

"We answer to Craven, that is all that matters."

"A captain? That does not mean much in a place like this, for nearly every man passing by is his superior. This is why the Captain should take the promotion he is offered. It would give power and legitimacy. Think if we are stopped and questioned on the street, we work on the authority of a Captain, that is all. Many officers would be quite in their right to take charge of us."

"A general, perhaps, but no other can interfere with the business of another regiment."

"They can and they do."

But Charlie shrugged it off and was angrier that he seemed

more concerned with how they might look than he did about his own safety, as he risked his life without care or consideration.

"How can you care so much about what people think?"

"Because I will be remembered by those people. My legacy is not just the things that I do, but even more importantly is who knows about those things and how they speak of me."

"And that matters to you more than your life?"

"If it is my time to be struck by a cannon ball, then so be it, but I will not live in fear of what I cannot change."

She smiled, for she knew that was not true, as he fretted over so many things which he could not affect.

They went on. Officers went back and forth between the various lodgings that were serving as barracks and headquarters. The busiest were the larger properties which also were fortunate enough to have fireplaces, the most valuable luxury in the bitter winter.

"What are we looking for? Craven's contest is not until later this afternoon."

"General Le Marchant is famed for his instruction and training, and I cannot imagine a morning would go by that he does not have his cavalrymen conducting exercises."

"Have you not seen enough marching and parading to last a lifetime? Most soldiers avoid it at all costs."

"A shame, for it does them so much good, and is a great spectacle."

"You think marching is good for you?" she laughed.

"Of course, men need discipline, and to act quickly in a structured manner when need be."

"And yet Craven rarely instructs us to do so."

"We are no mere line infantry regiment, are we? Our role

is something quite of its own, though we spend enough time in the saddle that we could certainly benefit some training by the likes of the General."

"We train with the sword, and I wouldn't have it any other way."

"So does the General."

He stopped as he could hear the sound of galloping horses and then the distant roar of orders being shouted, followed by the blowing of trumpets.

"Come on!" he yelled enthusiastically as he ran on with the boyish enthusiasm of a ten-year-old rushing to see an army parade.

They ran on and came to an embankment and a field beyond where cavalrymen galloped about in practice. Some were practicing complex manoeuvres whilst others cut against targets as they rode on by. Their targets were straw stuffed figures in old, faded uniforms, and their swords were made of wood. Charlie focused on Paget and marvelled at his endearing fixation on the display which lit up his eyes.

* * *

"It's time," declared Matthys.

Craven nodded in agreement as he got up and gathered up his sword belt.

"It is a pleasant surprise to be summoned for a friendly contest and not a real one," declared Matthys.

"Absolutely, I am here for the show," added Moxy.

They stepped out into the street to filthy looks from two

passing officers. For they had a ragged appearance in comparison to the well-dressed senior officers who occupied the town. Even so, they heard one of the men utter Craven's name with a mix of fear and disgust as they went past. They went on in the same direction Paget and Charlie had done hours before as they followed the sounds of galloping horses, the cry of officers' words of command, and the trumpet or bugle calls echoing out across all of the small village. They soon reached the field to find Charlie watching on alone, and then they spotted Paget, not in the audience, but on his horse Augustus. He darted between targets, striking at them as he went through Le Marchant's exercises with a beaming smile and complete focus and concentration.

"I couldn't hold him back," admitted Charlie.

"Has he given a good showing?" Craven asked.

"Of course."

Paget finished the course before saluting to several of those conducting the training with him. He galloped up before Craven with a triumphant and proud expression.

"A most interesting and rewarding exertion, Sir!"

He still held the wooden practice sabre in hand. It was an exact match for the light cavalry sabre Le Marchant had designed along with Henry Osborn all those years earlier and was not seen throughout the army in more than just the hands of light cavalrymen. The hardwood training sword was the same length, curvature, and flared tip of the blade which provided the cleaving power of the sabre. The only metal component was the ward iron which was in the same P shape pattern as the regulation swords. It looked like an unforgiving training tool, lacking the hand protection of the singlesticks commonly used by Craven and by fencers and cudgellers for centuries. The blade too was not designed to strike lightly, but with the same force as the live sharp blade.

"Ah, Captain Craven!" Le Marchant rode up beside Paget.

"Sir," acknowledged Craven.

"I was told you were not a man to arrive promptly, and yet I knew that a wager and the allure of the duel would motivate you."

"You seem to rather know me rather well, Sir."

"And I should know you better, of which I am certain to attain when we cross swords. Are you ready?"

"I am."

Le Marchant pointed to one of his men who rode up beside them and dismounted, passing the reins to Craven who looked confused.

"You would fight on horseback?"

"Captain, is it men of the cavalry and not the men of the infantry who are supplied with swords?"

"Sadly," croaked Craven.

"You have fought many battles from the saddle, have you not?"

"A few," admitted Craven.

"Come on then, man, up you go," insisted Le Marchant.

Craven looked up to see the anticipation of Paget's face, and he knew he could not let the Lieutenant down, nor shy away from a fight, especially after all of the anticipation. He mounted the horse and made himself comfortable.

"Here, Sir." Paget passed the wooden training sabre to the Captain.

Craven took it from him. The grip was still warm and well-shaped just like the steel versions, and yet the blade was very tip heavy, more so than Le Marchant's sword which he had admired the night before. The wooden swords were longer, in line with the regulation troopers' sabres, and they had even more mass, feeling more like a club than a sword to him.

"You don't much like your hands?" Craven lifted the hilt and marvelled at his exposed hand with only the thin ward iron to protect it.

"A man who cannot protect his hands has no business wielding a sword," replied Le Marchant sternly.

Craven shrugged. He had used so-called stirrup hilt sabres many times, and had long carried one for certain uses, but it was not something he ever used in practice sessions.

"Shall we say the first to win three exchanges or unhorse his opponent?"

"Why not?" Craven replied rhetorically.

Le Marchant turned and galloped away with such grace it was as if he had been born in the saddle. Some of the men began to cheer as a crowd of more than fifty cavalrymen watched on.

"Come on, Craven!" Charlie shouted.

The two mounted officers faced off against one another from twenty yards in a scene more reminiscent of the ancient sport of jousting, much to the amusement of the crowd who watched on. There was a brief moment which appeared like a whole minute as the two swordsmen weighed each other up. The pressure was huge. Neither had seen one another fight and did not know what to expect. And yet they were about to cross swords for the first time in a contest before an audience who would quickly spread news of it throughout the army. There was a lot at stake for both men in terms of reputation. Craven was also well aware of just how brutal the wooden sword could hit. It had all the weight of a cavalry sabre, and the horse's momentum could propel them to skull splitting speed.

Le Marchant spurred his horse forward. Craven matched him so that they closed distance just offset from one another as if they were on rails. They would then pass on each other's right side where the sword had most reach to both protect and strike from. Le Marchant confidently held his blade vertically in the way one salutes. He lifted at the wrist at the last moment and directed his blade so that it was nearly parallel to the ground and extended out in front of his face.

Craven waited to parry, not wanting to risk mistiming an attack and to be struck himself, whether he landed his own blow or not. Le Marchant's lifting of his blade was subtle and efficient so as to not expose his forearm, and the blade then came descending rapidly. Craven placed his wooden sabre in place for defence, and yet the General's strike hit with such tremendous force it was as if a battering ram had indeed struck him. His own sword was driven against his body which hurt, but it also braced the wooden sword to allow it to stay in place and take the force of the cut directed against him. The air was knocked out of Craven as he rocked back in the saddle. He barely stayed on the horse as Le Marchant vanished from sight as he galloped on.

For a few seconds the Captain was stunned and disorientated, but he could hear his friends crying out in support and that brought him around. He continued on and wheeled his horse about to prepare for the next pass to find Le Marchant was waiting patiently for him to collect himself. He acted like a gentleman, but he hit like a brutish ruffian, the sort you would never want to meet on the street at night. He quickly replayed their first clash in his mind and realised there was no trickery in Le Marchant's attack. He merely struck with immense speed and precision and a great deal of power behind it all. It was quite something to behold and was all the evidence Craven needed of the General's skill in the saddle. He knew he needed to reduce the pace of the fight. He had fought in the saddle many times out of necessity, but he had never truly mastered it. Against a regular cavalryman his skills had been thus far sufficient, but the difference in skill was clear to him to see and feel. A cut had opened on his forehead where his wooden sabre had been jammed against his head. It did not count as a blow landed, for Le Marchant's blade never touched him, but it certainly felt as though it had.

Once more the horses were spurred on, but this time Craven wheeled and caused the pace to slow as they approached. He feinted towards Le Marchant's right side before lashing a cut about onto the other side. Le Marchant's response was quite extraordinary. He quickly turned the sabre with a manipulation of his fingers so that his thumb rested on the side of the grip over the ears. His edge and guard were now directed away from Craven's blow, and he took the cut on the inside curve of the back of the sabre, where it was thickest and strongest on a steel version. The more than two inches of curve to the blade also acted like a scoop to trap Craven's blade for a moment before Le Marchant snapped a cut to the side of his head. The blow was nothing as savage as the first which had been delivered at the gallop, but it still smarted and opened another cut, stunning Craven for a moment. Le Marchant saluted with his sword and rode away to take up position for yet another pass.

Once more Craven slowed the pace, and they came to

blows again. This time Craven threw only half committed blows so that he could ensure he could parry and counter what came back at him. And they soon did, but as Le Marchant cast a thrust towards him, he parried it away to his right and lifted his sabre over Le Marchant's. It gave a slash across the General's chin. His head snapped a little from the blow before he exercised his jaw and smiled at the pain he had been caused, before saluting once more.

Now he was truly enjoying himself, for he knew it would be competitive as he had hoped. On the next pass Craven tried with all his speed and might to get Le Marchant's seemingly exposed sword arm, it being protected by such a small ward iron, but every blow was parried away with ease. He could see Le Marchant's continually changing and shifting his grip on his sword in between parries, cuts, and thrusts, giving a great precision and dexterity to his blows. After several parries, Craven saw his opening.

He smiled as he reached for his cut against Le Marchant's sword arm, but the General directed his horse forward and raised his hilt. He dropped the tip of his blade over his right shoulder, taking the cut in what seemed a most uncomfortable and unnatural position. Yet it stopped Craven's attack with ease and set up a perfect back handed blow which struck Craven's ribs with a heavy impact.

They reset their positions for another pass, which Craven knew would be their last if he could not land a blow. He did everything he could to adapt to Le Marchant as they came to blows. Attack after attack was exchanged between the two in a marvellous display of skill. As the horses slowed to an almost stop, Craven was able to apply more pressure, and Le Marchant was struggling to get to each parry and determine which of the Captain's attacks were feints and which were attacks.

"Come on, Sir!" Paget cried out with excitement from the sidelines as it seemed as if the Captain was about to even the score. But Le Marchant moved his horse on with precision to move around to Craven's rear left side where he was most exposed and would have the hardest time defending. The Captain did not have the horsemanship skills to respond as quickly. Le Marchant stood up in the saddle as if to make a tremendous blow onto Craven's head, and yet he was not even in distance to do so. As Craven's blade went up to parry, the General quickly struck a blow down onto his thigh. A cheer rang out from the ground as well as laughter. Craven had fallen foul of a weakness he was not so accustomed to, that he could not move his legs in his own defence as he could when fighting on foot.

"Well done. You hit like a hammer," conceded Craven as the two men rode back to the crowd. Le Marchant raised his hand and called for silence.

"You have won, Sir," declared Craven.

But Le Marchant shook his head.

"A fine contest indeed, and I thank you for that, but I am a cavalryman, and we fought my game. Now let us fight yours."

Craven didn't know what to say.

"Or would you not like a second crack at me?" Le Marchant smiled as he leapt from his horse and stepped away into open ground with his wooden sabre still in hand.

"Go on, Sir!" Paget insisted.

He did not need to be told twice. He was being offered a chance to do what he did best. He leapt from the horse and rushed out onto the open field where the General awaited him. The two men came to guard, and never was the difference so clear to see between each man. Le Marchant was standing in a casual upright position with his feet close together, and his left arm in front of his waist at the same position he used from horseback. He looked like a cavalryman in the training exercises they practiced on their feet before ever getting into the saddle. For a beginner would invariably cut his horse's neck and ears if not training correctly before attempting it.

Craven looked just as comfortable, but in a posture perfectly suited to fighting on foot. His feet were well spaced and his knees well bent, his lead shoulder propelled forward, and his left kept well back as to give him maximum reach and protection. His left hand was tucked away against his hip so that it did not get in the way nor risk injury.

Cheers rang out in support of both men as they cautiously approached one another. Craven probed at his opponent's defences with small jabs of his point to provoke a response. It soon came. Le Marchant launched a heavy cut, though without the horse to double his strength, it was quite manageable in the parry. Craven took the blow on a hanging position, his hilt raised and tip low so that Le Marchant's blade slid down it. Craven feinted a riposte to his head in the same blow that had just come for him, but as Le Marchant moved to parry, he realised his mistake too late. He had fallen into Craven's trap. The wood sabre crashed into the General's flank, and he winced in pain as he doubled over briefly before recomposing himself. He seemed to be enjoying the experience even more than the battle of horseback, embracing the difficult contest wholeheartedly.

They went at it again in a second pass. Le Marchant's cuts

came in thick and fast. He presented no openings with which to time his attacks, but neither did he have the speed on his feet to close with Craven when he needed to. The Captain darted in and out with supreme footwork. As he moved back and forth, he slipped his leg out of many of the blows and traversed away from others. He used his footwork to run circles around Le Marchant, just as the General had used his riding skill and horse to do the same in their previous contest.

Le Marchant could see the skill before his eyes, and yet he gave it his all. But soon enough Craven tricked him with a cut that upon landing was turned and directed into a thrust, the curvature carrying the point around his guard and landing on his chest. He withdrew and saluted before starting again. For a moment he took the same relaxed guard he had before, but he then leapt forward like a racehorse. He gave out a loud war cry and rained in blows as he kept running forward, finally making a great sweep for Craven's legs. He had progressed so far forward and so quickly that Craven's slip did not clear himself from the blade which lashed into his thigh.

The two men separated and came to guard once more. Le Marchant knew it could be the last exchange if he lost, just as Craven had known in their mounted exchange. And so, he came forward aggressively again, using the same aggression and speed that had resulted in his only success in the fight. He went forward with speed and precision, but Craven did not back away and attempted to maintain distance this time, instead meeting the aggression head on. He parried a strong blow and leapt forward into close range with the General. He grasped the guard of his opponent's sword and ripped it from the hand which held it. This disarmed Le Marchant as he directed the point of his sword to the General's chest.

Le Marchant merely smiled in response. He stepped away and began to clap in appreciation. His cavalrymen did the same, for it had been a sublime display to behold, with both men leaving with their honour and dignity not just intact, but elevated. Le Marchant strode forward and wrapped his arms about Craven in a firm embrace, leading him back to the crowd which still cheered with excitement.

"You are all that I had hoped for, Captain," declared Le Marchant.

"A better rider I have never crossed swords with," admitted Craven.

"Then perhaps there is much we can learn from one another."

The mood of the audience who had come out to support both men was of amazement and respect.

A rider galloped onto the scene and approached Le Marchant with some urgency. He handed him a message, which he read quickly. He tried to keep his composure, but it was clear to them all that the messenger brought some significant news.

"The games are over. It seems we have work to do," he smiled.

"What of our wager?"

"We are three to one in each encounter. It seems to me that we have a draw."

"And what does that mean?"

"You have earned the right to make the decision yourself, Captain. I don't know what the best path for you would be, and I think you probably have a better idea yourself. Good luck, Craven."

Le Marchant shook the Captain's hand and made to hurry away.

"Something big is happening, isn't it?" Craven thought of the message that had prompted the General to leave so rapidly.

"Merry Christmas," replied Le Marchant.

"And to you, Sir."

They parted ways on good terms as Craven returned to some of his closest friends.

"That was marvellous, Sir," insisted Paget.

"He is one hell of a rider. Pray we never meet his kind in a Frenchman, for they will quite literally run circles around us."

"Then we must train more."

Craven nodded in agreement.

"How many days until Christmas?"

"Why it is tomorrow, Sir." Paget was surprised at his question.

"Then let us gather our horses, for I would spend it with the Salfords."

CHAPTER 10

Ferreira sat solemnly playing cards in the corner of a barn with several of his compatriots. A great many of the Salfords had squeezed into the modest space. Their sheer number was at least keeping the room warm enough to be comfortable, but the mood was low, until the door was thrown open and Craven stormed in carrying a keg.

"Get your fill, lads!"

They roared with elation as Charlie and Moxy followed him in with more barrels. Ferreira leapt to his feet to greet them, as any excitement was a welcome break. The prospects of a bleak Christmas was a disheartening affair, especially as the day was only a matter of hours away. Matthys and Ellis came in carrying legs of cured meat on either shoulder, drawing another roar, but as Ferreira approached, he looked at the back of the keg Craven had just set down to see some writing on the rear of it.

"Property of…" he began.

Craven's hand reached around and covered the words before he could read them.

"Of James Craven," he smiled, as both of them knew it was not true.

The drink soon flowed.

"Well? What news?"

"It was not what we expected, but something is coming soon, that much I am certain of," he replied mysteriously before climbing onto a rickety old table that had been dragged inside.

The troops quickly came to silence as many pointed towards the Captain. They all watched and listened with curiosity for some news, but mostly just relieved to see him returned and with generous gifts. He took a deep breath and went on.

"First of all, I want to say what a privilege it is to have you all by my side, and for me to stand beside you."

Cheers rang out.

"It's a tough time of year, and it's been a hard year, but we are still here. We are still standing, and I promise you, next year we will spend Christmas in Madrid!"

Cries of excitement rang out.

"Thank you all, and Merry Christmas!"

The drink soon flowed, and for several more days it went on as they somehow found enough food and drink to make merry without rest for days on end. Until one evening when it had all gotten a little overwhelming for Paget, and Craven could see it.

"Do you want to take a walk?"

"Why yes, Sir, I think that is an excellent idea."

Matthys couldn't help but be impressed by Craven's sense

of duty towards his friends in a way he had always hoped to see but could not have imagined possible. He watched them leave before going on to find a drink.

The crisp evening air was indeed a welcome treat after the stale barn filled with sweaty soldiers.

"What is on your mind?"

"Nothing, and everything," admitted Paget.

Craven smiled and nodded along.

"You know what I mean, Sir?"

"Not really, I have always been better at focusing on one thing entirely, perhaps too much some would say."

"Is that what I should do, Sir?"

"I wish I knew, but you should ask Matthys, for I am sure he will have a far more useful answer for you."

Paget groaned.

"You are still thinking about the assault of the fortress, aren't you?"

"Yes, Sir, how can I not? It will be a most momentous occasion, and if we succeed, it will be talked about for many years to come, centuries even."

"And you want to be a part of it?"

"Yes, Sir. It will be a most incredible thing to stand triumphantly upon those walls."

"You want to be hailed as a hero?"

"I want to be a hero for my country."

Craven shook his head as some of Paget's ideals were still unchanging since the first day they met years previously.

"Is it such a silly thing to desire, Sir?"

"It sounds it to me, but I don't think any man should be able to tell another what they should and should not desire.

Some men never pick up a sword their entire lifetime, and I could never understand a man like that, but I do not decry them for it. For they probably think I am just as strange as I think they are."

"Then it is all a matter of perspective?"

Craven nodded in agreement as they walked out to the perimeter of the camp where it was quiet and dark and most peaceful. They could look up at the stars and appreciate the tranquil scenery. The sound of thousands of soldiers busy chatting was a distant muffled tone, and they were far enough away from the fires to feel they were truly amongst nature. They passed by several dilapidated old barns, which were not even sturdy enough to be patched up by the troops as shelter, for they were crumpling into nothing.

Craven stopped and took a seat on a collapsing section of wall which was down below waist height.

"My mind wanders too much when there is so little to do, Sir."

"That much I can understand, but there is more to life than soldiering."

"I am not sure your life is for me," declared Paget.

"No, I suppose it might not be, but you can forge your own life."

"Perhaps when all of this is over, and there is no more need for an army in the Peninsula. I imagine the need for men such as us will soon vanish as quickly as it arrived."

"I don't think the need for fighting men ever truly goes away. Perhaps they might let go the idle and useless ones, and make sure those officers who are fat and old are sent to live a comfortable life back in England, but there will always be work for men like us, so long as we can keep doing it."

"And when we cannot?"

"Pray we have amassed enough wealth that we can live an easy life."

Paget frowned as that touched another nerve.

"I fear I had that and had only to keep my father happy to ensure I led as comfortable a life as he has."

"Is that why you want to lead an assault? You think getting your name in the papers or mentioned in despatches might put you back in your father's good graces?"

"I know it would. For he would much like to brag about me and would seem most foolish and disingenuous to the men of his standing if he did not support a war hero in Wellington's army."

"You worry about getting back into your father's good graces, but I think he should be more concerned with getting back into yours."

"He is my father."

"And you would accept his gratitude after what he has done?"

"He is family, and it is not easy to walk away from a fortune. I could have everything a man could ever want if I could regain his trust and respect."

"And what will it cost you?"

"Cost? My father has not need of more money."

"Not in coin, but your soul."

"I thought you did not believe in any of that, Sir?"

"I believe there is much of us that we can lose and have to give up."

Paget sighed and groaned. He was starting to understand

the Captain's meaning. There was a brief lull in their conversation as everything fell remarkably silent, and in that moment, they heard a small stone drop nearby. Craven spun around and noticed a glimmer of movement between two of the ruined structures. He shot to his feet as his hand reached over and took a firm grasp of his sword in readiness to draw.

"Who goes there?"

Paget looked confused but moved back to join the Captain's side, trusting in his instincts.

"What is it, Sir?" Paget whispered.

Craven would not reply as he was pinpoint focused on what he perceived as a threat.

"More wolves?" Paget asked anxiously, as he had witnessed what the opportunistic devils could do to a man. But still Craven would not reply as he shook his head to demand silence, but that only made Paget more anxious, seeing the genuine concern on Craven's face.

A cloaked and hooded figure stepped out a little from the shadows of the structures, causing Paget to almost jump out of his skin. It was a man of a good build, and the glimmer of moonlight shimmered from a sword which he had drawn and in hand. It was enough to prompt Craven to draw his own blade and Paget quickly followed.

"Identify yourself," demanded Craven.

For what felt like a full minute the figure did not move, and they could just see the condensation of their breath in the cold night air. Yet only a few seconds had passed, but the figure was most intimidating, as if an ethereal being had entered their presence.

"Who are you?"

Another anxious silence ensued before the figure finally spoke.

"You know who I am."

Craven would recognise the man's French accent any time, for it had long haunted his dreams. "Bouchard," he snarled.

Paget almost stopped breathing at the revelation. They had thought Craven's nemesis long gone, either dead or retired.

"You want to be beaten again?" Craven snapped.

"You have never beaten me, and that fact plagues you to this day, does it not?"

"Your hold over me is lost, do your worst," hissed Craven.

Bouchard came toward them, seemingly happy to oblige and not caring that he was outnumbered. He appeared to be alone, yet as he closed into distance, he pulled away his cloak to reveal he was carrying some object in his left hand about the size of a tankard and carried the same way by a handle on the side. He reached over to it with his left and twisted the top, causing a window to open in the front and reveal it was a dark lantern. A lamp with a cover which allowed a man to conceal himself in the dark until the right moment, and then use the directional light as a weapon to those devious enough to do so. It was the tool of a thief and a murderer.

The light shone brightly, and the night vision of both Craven and Paget was blown out for a moment before they could adjust. Craven directed his blade forward and began to make revolutions in a circular motion as to find any target which came close to him. But he felt his sword be beaten down before he leapt back at the inevitable strike which would follow it. He felt the very tip of a blade slice into his chin, and he stumbled back, crashing to the ground. He was quick to get back to his feet as he tried to shield his eyes from the light and see what was going on ahead.

He could just make out Paget struggling against the blinding light, and he even managed to land a thrust against Bouchard between his lantern and sword, but the blade stopped dead as though it had been thrust against a wall rather than entering the Frenchman's body. Bouchard looked unaffected, and he struck Paget on the head with the pommel of his sword. It sent him crashing lifelessly down to the ground.

Craven leapt back to his feet and closed the distance but quickly found the lantern being directed at his face once again. His vision had adjusted a little to it, but it was still obscuring much of the Frenchman's movement as he moved the lantern from side to side and above his head. Craven lost sight of his opponent's blade in the disorientation of the trick, and he could see now why Paget's sword had done nothing. The devious Frenchman wore a close-fitting cuirass armour about his torso that had stopped Paget's blade from penetrating. Craven looked disgusted by the tricks.

"This is what you need to beat me? These cheap tricks?"

"You have never fought a fair fight in your life," seethed Bouchard.

"Neither have I," said another voice in the darkness, causing Bouchard to turn in horror at the prospect of another joining the contest. Timmerman charged out from the shadows, but not with a sword in hand, but a nine-foot-long Sergeant's spontoon, a heavy bladed half pike more akin to a boar spear than anything else. Timmerman thrust the heavy polearm towards the Frenchman, holding it firm in both hands as he thrust. The blade glanced off Bouchard's armour, and the Frenchman dropped his blade behind the prongs that reached out either side below the spear-like blade. They were intended to stop the huge weapon from penetrating too deeply against an enemy that they might strike back at the user, just as a boar spear did, but Bouchard wrenched back against them and ripped the weapon from the Major's hands. However, Timmerman was not deterred. He drew out his sabre, took off his cloak, and quickly wound it around his left arm to use in both attack and defence.

"The bastard has a breast plate on," declared Craven.

"Then we shall have to take his head," smiled Timmerman as the two officers nodded to one another, knowing exactly what the other was thinking.

They began to circle their man so that not only could they strike from different angles, but the directional light of the dark lantern could only face one of them at a time. Timmerman leapt forward and initiated the attack. Craven followed suit so that they attacked simultaneously and gave the Frenchman no chance of dealing with them individually. He began to whirl about, swinging wildly in circles to keep them both at bay. Timmerman backed away, but not to flee in fear. He chose his moment carefully as he unravelled his cloak from his arm and tossed it towards the lantern wielding arm of Bouchard, covering it completely. He then leapt forward and cut down at the cloak covered arm and lantern. Bouchard gave out a cry as his hand was struck, and he dropped the device, which smashed to the floor. It quickly set Timmerman's cloak alight, brightening the whole scene for all to behold.

A groan rang out from Paget as he was coming around, and when he saw Bouchard he shot to his feet, ready to fight again. Bouchard weighed up his options before growling angrily and turned to flee without a word. Timmerman went to go after him, but Craven stepped into his path and stopped him.

"No, do not fight on his terms, for he will have all manner of traps and tricks awaiting you." Timmerman looked stunned that the Captain would even care for his wellbeing, "What were you even doing out here?"

"Hunting that bastard," replied Timmerman as he watched his cloak burn before picking up the spontoon he had brought to the fight.

"You knew he was here?"

"Not for certain, but I had my suspicions."

"Based on what?"

"I've tried to kill you, too, Craven. I think I know more than most men about how it might be achieved," he smirked.

"Never succeeded though, did you?" Craven joked.

"No, and I am rather glad of that, for I think I might have been a man without a purpose had I ever achieved it."

"That was Bouchard," declared Paget who rubbed his sore head.

"Yes, it was," replied Craven.

"And you did not go after him, Sir?"

"I won't play his games."

"Is that a Sergeant's spontoon?" Paget was marvelling at the huge hardwood shaft with steel blade atop it, which no officer had carried since his grandfather's days in the army.

"If you want to hunt an animal, you take the right tools for the job."

"Not that it did you a lot of good."

"Bouchard is a slippery son of a bitch, but I will get to

him," smiled Timmerman.

"Why? Why do you even care?" Craven asked in surprise.

"Because that French bastard hunts Englishmen, and that won't do at all."

"When have you ever cared about Englishmen?" Paget snapped at him.

"What were you like before you met Craven?"

"A pain in the arse," smiled Craven endearingly. Paget could not deny it and was quite proud of that fact, "If Bouchard is back, he will not stop."

"No, and neither will we," added Timmerman.

Craven went to walk away but stopped beside Timmerman and put a hand on his shoulder.

"It's nice to be surprised sometimes."

"I am sure Bouchard thought so."

"I was talking about you. I don't trust you, but Paget always tells me that all men can change. Keep this up, and I might start believing him."

Craven walked on, leaving Timmerman looking out into the night with a great big smile on his face. He had much enjoyed the evening, and it was a joy to be around Craven once more, for he had missed his old rival.

The drinking at the barn went on until the New Year was nearing, being just hours away, and yet all of the food and drink was gone. Matthys stepped inside the barn that had become their home for a little while as he searched for Craven and the other officers. They were sitting playing cards with Ferreira and the Portuguese officers.

"They say Wellington says the army will be ready to march on Ciudad Rodrigo in ten days," he said quietly as he leaned in over Craven's shoulder.

"Then the time has finally come?" Ferreira asked.

"Has it? A lot can happen in ten days," replied Craven cynically.

"The General would not have us march in the bitter winter weather," insisted Paget.

Craven nodded in agreement.

"Ten days and all the liquor is gone," complained Craven.

"Gone, did you say?" roared a voice at the doorway as Major Harcourt Doyle appeared before them and held the door open. Several of his gunners carried in supplies to cheers from all.

"How?"

"You were there when we needed you, Captain, and I will return the favour, but don't you forget it, you hear?"

"Never."

"And we're staying to join in the festivities!"

"I love you," replied Craven with a smile.

"How could you not?" Doyle laughed.

Matthys smiled as he watched them all indulge in not just the drinking but in good natured banter as the evening went on. The war felt like it was finally progressing, and they would all give anything to break the monotony, even if that meant marching against the enemy and taking all the risks associated with it. The partying went on into the early hours until most of them collapsed asleep where they had been sitting or fallen as they made the most of the night in good spirits.

The next thing Craven knew there was a heavy banging on the barn door, which could not open as Doyle lay sprawled out across the entrance and blocking it. Craven tried to get up and staggered back and forth before finding his balance. He pulled Doyle from the door, and it soon burst open. An excited Paget fell in looking more excitable than normal, even for him. Craven was thrown back and nearly fell as the door drove him back. He tripped over Doyle who groaned as he came around from Craven's kick, and the Captain went tumbling.

Both of them slowly got up as Paget waited with anticipation to share the news and could finally not contain himself anymore. Craven was blinded by the bright light invading their space through the open doorway. The night had brought fresh snowfall which the morning light glistening from.

"It's happening, Sir, it's happening!" Paget cried in an excited outburst.

"What's happening?" Matthys demanded, as he awoke in a better state than most of them.

"Wellington has ordered the march to Ciudad Rodrigo!"

"When?" Doyle asked.

"Now, today!"

Craven groaned in despair, for he was in no state for such soldiering. "And do we have orders?"

"Yes, you do!" Major Spring stepped in after Paget.

Craven rolled his eyes in disappointment. He already had a good idea of what was coming next, and he knew he wouldn't like it.

"Captain, the army moves on, but the French will do everything in their power to retard our advance. I want you and your boys to go ahead and make their work difficult. Make it hell for them."

"Don't you have cavalry for that?"

"We do, Major Doyle. Some are already out there with

more departing, but Craven has a unique ability to cause absolute chaos."

"Never has a truer statement been uttered, Sir," replied Paget.

Craven shrugged in agreement. "When do we leave?"

"There is no time to waste, Captain. The French have moved troops out of Ciudad Rodrigo to assist at Valencia, and it will be many weeks or even months before they can be reinforced. Wellington would have us take the fortress before the damned French can gather their strength."

"And the equipment for a siege? Ladders, gabions, all the things required for a siege?"

"All ready, for we have had hundreds of men preparing them in secret at Almeida. We have what we need, Captain, but we need a path all the way into Spain."

"I can do that," Craven smiled, and he was relieved to finally have some purpose.

"And Bouchard, Sir?" Paget asked in concern.

"He is back?" Spring asked.

"He is," admitted Craven.

"Deal with him, Craven," seethed Spring as he passed him his orders and headed for the door but stopped short.

"Oh, and one last thing, congratulations, Major Craven."

"Thank you, Sir."

The room was silent for just a moment as the hung-over troops took a while for the meaning to set in, but they soon leapt to their feet and cheered in celebration of his promotion.

"All right, all right!" he roared as he calmed them down, "I want every man ready to march in one hour! Leave nothing behind!"

The news of the promotion and that they were finally advancing into Spain invigorated every soldier in the room. They burst into action, and chatter filled the room as they enthusiastically discussed what the next weeks would bring whilst they readied themselves to march.

"Well done, Sir," congratulated Paget.

"Don't think this means you will be Captain anytime soon," he smiled.

"I wouldn't dream of it, Sir."

"Yes, you would," smirked Craven before the Lieutenant rushed on to gather his things.

"I didn't think I'd ever see the day." Doyle slowly staggered out after Major Spring, knowing he had his work cut out. Ferreira was the only one who did not get to work and leaned in over an empty barrel beside Craven.

"You finally did it? You have become what you always ran from," he muttered.

"I came here to your country for my own reasons, but this is about more than just me now. If I have to take promotion to protect what we have, then so be it." He groaned to prove he still didn't want it.

"Dining with generals and now getting promotions? Before long you'll be seeking a title and living like royalty," Ferreira smiled back at him.

"They'd never have me."

"Don't sell yourself short. You've achieved a lot of things many people said you never would."

Craven nodded in appreciation.

"And you also, for it seems this damned war has finally made soldiers of both of us."

Ferreira shrugged as if he didn't agree.

"I've personally seen you do as much as any soldier in this army. You can hide behind that persona all you like, but you are a damned fine officer and an even better fighter."

"Don't think because you are now a Major that you need to lay down praise to motivate us."

"I meant it. Many of us never intended to walk this road, but here we are, and I admit I am glad to be on it with you."

"I think you are going soft."

Craven laughed as he nodded in agreement. Timmerman strode in, and the mood changed immediately as they went on the defensive.

"The army moves out, do you?" he enquired.

"We do, and our orders are to sweep any French from the road to Ciudad Rodrigo and the surrounding area, will you join us?" Craven answered him.

Timmerman slammed his hand down on the rickety table they had used for their drinks the night before, and it collapsed under his violent blow.

"Damn right, I am! It's about time we went East!" He turned about and strode away without another word, laughing maniacally.

"Why did you not tell Major Spring about what happened with Bouchard?" Paget had joined them.

Ferreira took it as his cue to leave and went on his business, leaving Craven to answer to the young man, to whom he did not have to give an answer, but he certainly felt the young man deserved one.

"Bouchard is my problem, and I will deal with him."

"But he came remarkably close. He tried to assassinate

you, and he could have tried the same against any officer in this army, up to and including Lord Wellington himself."

"Yes, he did, which tells you how desperate he is."

"Desperate? How so, Sir?"

"He knows we no longer fear him, and he had to resort to tricks, which means it is he who lives in fear."

Paget thought about the sentiment and struggled to smile at the prospect. The danger the French ghost posed was still very real, and he still had the headaches from the blow he had been dealt as proof of it. Craven led him outside into the fresh snow so that he may see the scenes of chaos for himself. Everywhere he looked he could see soldiers moving back and forth with a determination. They did not rush, but they went about their business with an organised military discipline, eager to get the blood flowing in the cold weather and to finally make their advance. Wagons were drawn along the roads and artillery pieces hooked up to their limbers in the distance. The whole place had come alive, and it was just one small village of which there would be so many more in the tens of miles of which the army had been spread to last out the winter.

"We will deal with Bouchard, I promise you that," vowed Craven.

CHAPTER 11

The march East from the winter cantonments and lodgings in local villages and towns had been met with a great excitement, but the reality of the bitter cold weather had quickly dampening spirits as the troops struggled on through icy winds and the most awful of conditions.

"I hope and pray Lord Wellington knows what he is doing," whispered Paget as he rode beside Craven.

"Men will die on this road, but it is all a calculated risk."

"How so, Sir?" Paget could not imagine how the cost would be worth it.

"Lose a small number now, but far less at the fortress we will soon assault."

"You believe Wellington would be so callous?"

"It is the very opposite. For he tries to save men from the very worst of it, and it will be terrible, I promise you that."

But Paget would not be convinced as he imagined himself

the hero of the assault, and the rewards and restoration of his reputation and wealth which would inevitably follow.

"She worries about you, you know that?" Craven looked back at Charlie, who seemed least bothered by the harsh conditions, for they were nothing as bad as the worst of days she had lived through. Paget looked back, too, and knew precisely what the newly appointed Major meant and to whom he was referring.

"And I her," he replied.

"You care what your father thinks of you, a man who has disowned you and sits comfortably by a fire thousands of miles away, whilst she fights beside you here, does she not deserve as much consideration, if not more?"

"But she is just a…" began Paget.

"Just a soldier? Just a commoner like me?"

Paget scoffed as he was embarrassed and could find no answers.

"Do you love her?" Craven asked directly.

"How could I not?"

Craven nodded in agreement.

"What do you want from me?"

"If this war has taught me anything, then it is that no man is an island. I lived my life like that once for a very long time, but I was wrong."

"What are you saying?"

"That she is every part of your life. Your health, your love, and your future."

"And what are you saying I must do?"

"Stop undervaluing it. Your father withholds money from you, but Charlie gives you everything, and she only wants one thing in return, to know that you are safe."

"How can a soldier be safe when he marches to war? We drive into Spain, and we hunt the French. All the odds are against us. You heard General Le Marchant. We cannot win this war. We can only lose it in the most honourable way possible."

"Le Marchant is a good man, and he has some impressive skills, but that does not make him right."

"No, Sir?" Paget questioned.

"He has only just entered this war, but for men like us we have been here for years. We have seen what this war is and what each side is capable of."

"But is Spain all but in the hands of the enemy? I hear the last cities will fall within weeks."

"And yet all across Spain people still fight. Let us worry about Ciudad Rodrigo, for that is the obstacle before us and all that matters now. If we can take that damned city, then we can go forward."

"And if we cannot?"

Craven shrugged as he knew it would likely spell disaster.

"It must be done, it must be," he insisted.

"Captain!" Moxy yelled, forgetting Craven's promotion, but nobody admonished him. The Welshman's horse reared up as he turned about and pointed over the ridge ahead.

"This is it! On me!"

Craven raced onwards at the head of all who were mounted and leaving those on foot in the dust. As they crested the ridge, they could see the target that Moxy was alerting them to. A scouting party of thirty French cavalrymen were looking back at them from two hundred yards away, looking to glean any information they could about troop movements and assess whether they had the numbers to engage against their British counterparts attempting to do the same. Craven brought them to an abrupt halt and surveyed the scene. Moxy took up his rifle and took aim at the Frenchmen who did not perceive a threat, but Moxy's rifle cracked into life and spurt flame, shooting one of the Frenchman from his saddle. Several of their horses reared up and staggered about all jittery as the French soldiers looked down at their fallen comrade in stunned disbelief. Craven drew out his sword.

"Major Spring asked us to clear the way, so let's clear it!"

He launched his horse forward, leading the others in a cavalry charge. The Frenchmen looked uncertain but drew out their swords nonetheless and finally came forward to join them. As they closed the distance, it was plain to see that the French morale was already low after the loss of their man to Moxy's rifle and by nature of them being outnumbered.

Craven remembered Le Marchant's methods as he approached his target who was moving far slower than him. He directed a cut at his man and made it simple, attempting to power through just as Le Marchant had. The blades made contact, and the Frenchman's arm buckled a little from the impact, but the back of his own sword was not driven into his face as Le Marchant done to Craven, and a back handed counter cut soon came for his neck. Craven lifted his hilt and dropped the tip of his sword over his right shoulder, just as Le Marchant had done. He took the cut on his blade behind and beyond his vision. He felt the heavy impact of the sabre strike his blade, but the energy was soon carried away as the Frenchman's sword slid down his own and fell safely away.

He was forced to quickly recover his blade to parry a heavy

blow aimed for his neck and stopped it dead before wheeling about. But he could see the fight in the Frenchmen was already collapsing as Paget ran one through and Amyn rode by another and cleaved with such a blow it was reminiscent of Le Marchant himself. It dealt such a horrific long slice against his target that the will of the enemy was truly broken. Many turned to flee before the order was even given. French cries to retreat soon followed. Several more were cut down, but the rest soon broke away and galloped from the scene as fast as they could. Birback dug in his heels to go after them.

"Hold!" Craven cried.

Birback reluctantly turned about and returned to them.

"They've had enough," declared Craven.

Matthys nodded in agreement. He then got down from his horse to look at the man Amyn had cloven almost in two with such an immense blow. It had not only struck hard but was also drawn far across the man's body.

"Was it necessary?"

Amyn didn't even know how to respond.

"Is this what we are? Butchers?"

"Would you say that to Le Marchant? For he would have done the same," replied Craven in the Mameluke's defence.

"Would he?"

"You're damned right he would have, and you know it."

"What I know is we brought a man here who butchers Christians like they are cattle."

"Enough! I won't hear any more of this, do you hear me?"

Matthys lowered his head and said nothing, not even the slightest recognition of Craven's orders.

"Gather anything useful."

"And the dead, Sir?" Paget asked.

"Our job is to sweep the enemy from these lands. There are plenty of men following who can deal with them."

Matthys looked even more disgusted at the prospect of leaving the bodies. He looked at the sliced open Frenchman just as Birback reached the body and looted the corpse heavy-handedly.

"How did it ever come to this?" Matthys muttered solemnly and openly in disgust.

Craven's anger at his sentiments were balanced by an equal measure of sorrow at seeing his old friend in such a way. For it was true that the war was at times truly awful, and Matthys being the kind soul he was, must surely have carried a greater burden of it than most. A whistling noise rang out, the familiar sound of a lead ball passing by, and Ellis was rocked slightly. The sound of a gunshot echoed out far into the distance, for the sound travelled far slower than the lead ball. They all looked to the quiet soul they had only recently begun to understand as he wheeled his horse about, as if he was okay, but as he did so they could see a hole in his coat high on his chest. He soon dropped unconscious and fell from the saddle, landing hard on the ground.

"Ellis!" Moxy leapt from his horse and rushed to his friend's side, for they had spent seemingly endless days by one another's side.

"Where did it come from?" Craven wheeled is horse about to looked for the origin of the attack. There was a faint wisp of smoke in the distance high up on rocky terrain.

"Ellis!" Moxy yelled again as he pulled him over to find his eyes were open.

"What happened?"

Moxy smiled, as if by some miracle he must be unharmed.

"Some bastard shot you," gushed Moxy, but the smile was soon gone as he placed a man on the hole in Ellis's coat. It was wet with blood. Matthys joined them as the two peeled open Ellis' jacket.

"On me!" Craven ordered.

Most of them drew their horses up close ready to go on, but Moxy and Matthys continued to stay by Ellis' side.

"Moxy, come on!" Craven shouted at him.

"No," Moxy looked up at him defiantly.

"That was an order!"

But Moxy would not move.

Craven dug his spurs in, and just as he moved, he heard another shot whiz past. It struck one of Ferreira's men, but the shot was clearly meant for him.

"This is madness. We have to do something," declared Hawkshaw as the Portuguese rifleman winced in pain, a shot lodged in his body.

"Moxy!" Craven shouted again.

The Welshman at last looked at him.

"We have a sharpshooter to deal with. There is nothing you can do for Ellis that Matthys cannot. Let's move and get him!"

Moxy didn't want to, but he could see both Matthys and Ellis wanted him to do as the Major asked. He grimaced before leaping back onto his horse, noting the foot element of the Salfords was now in sight and would soon reach their position.

"Let's get that bastard," he growled.

They rode on at great speed. Another shot soon landed,

though this time on Craven. However, it struck towards the edge of the shoulder of his greatcoat and left a deep groove impression, skimming off and away without any serious damage. They soon reached the base of the shallow rocky slope. Easy enough to traverse on foot, but it was completely impossible for their horses. Craven leapt from the saddle and just ran on, leaving his horse to wander. More than thirty of them ascended the slope as the occasional shot rang out. One man was hit and stayed in place, and another had a narrow miss as a ball struck the furniture of his rifle.

"This is what it must feel like to be the enemy," sniffled Paget as he thought of all the times they had waited in ambush for the French soldiers.

"Just keep your head down and keep moving!" Craven cried out.

Another lead ball struck a rock nearby and sent fragment blasting into Paget's face. He stopped to clear and recover his vision from the dust and debris with his left hand. Craven grabbed the Lieutenant and pulled him on further as they continued their ascent. Yet it was not long before Craven stopped and looked up, as something had changed.

"They have stopped firing," he declared.

"Could it be just one man?" Charlie asked.

"One or two, but no more, or they would be raining fire down upon us," added Moxy. He now had his head on straight and looked determined to hunt down the man who had shot his close friend.

"I don't like this," declared Ferreira.

Craven nodded in agreement.

"Then let us not run into trouble like fools." Craven

quickly surveyed the scene and could see a relatively even track of ground moving South around the hill.

"Ferreira, you take half of the men and keep advancing. You keep French heads down if you see them. Keep a steady pace but don't rush it, let us do this together. The rest of us will work our way around this slope and come up on their flank."

No more words needed to be spoken as everyone knew what they had to do. They divided themselves in roughly even forces of a little over fifteen soldiers each. It felt more than enough to have numerical superiority. Craven remained low and kept an eye on the top of the hill to try and ensure their movements were not noticed, but there was no sign of movement and so he hurried on.

"Sir, what is a sharpshooter doing out here all alone?" Paget asked.

"Assessing our troops movements, I should imagine."

"With just one or two men?"

"One or two men can hold up an entire column from marching onward. That is why Spring sent us out here, to clear this sort of trouble."

But Paget still did not look convinced as they scurried about the hillside. They finally began to climb to where they might get the high ground over the enemy, as Ferreira led the way from below.

"There." Charlie pointed to a vantage point ahead. Just below them two men lay in the prone position, well-hidden and concealed from those below, and just thirty yards away.

"Those rifles, look at them. American long rifles," whispered Paget in envious amazement as he looked at the long-barrelled weapons employed by their attackers.

"What are they doing in the hands of the French? They don't even use rifles," replied Craven.

"Let's take them off their hands, shall we?" Moxy said with a menacing smile. He rested his rifle and took aim whilst Charlie did the same. They waited for Craven's order, but he merely nodded to give the signal.

The two rifles cracked to life and ignited almost simultaneously, yet neither of their targets moved. No flinch in pain or panic, it was not the way a man responded to being shot, not even from most mortal of wounds.

"Did you miss?" Craven asked in disbelief, "Surely not." He took out his spyglass for a better look and could see for himself where the shots had landed. They were in the flanks and backs of each man.

"I don't like this, Sir," protested Paget.

"Perhaps Ferreira's boys hit them first?"

"And they just happened to fall dead in a firing position?"

Craven grimaced in frustration as he tried to figure it out just as Ferreira's unit made their final approach. They were soon on top of the bodies, turning them over to find they were not men at all, but merely stuffed uniforms posed to look like they were men.

"No!" Craven muttered, as he realised they had fallen into a trap, but far too late to do anything about it.

A line of twenty men rose up from behind some rocks a little over fifty yards from where Ferreira had found the manikins. They wore no uniforms and just a mix of dull earthy tones which concealed them well within the terrain.

"Get down!" Craven roared, but a volley suddenly rang out, although it was nothing like a musket volley. There was a crack of gunfire, albeit far quieter than they were used to with their black powder muskets and rifles. The volley was also entirely powderless, and yet the effect was no less devastating.

Ferreira himself was struck in the arm and three of his men went down. The Portuguese Captain swore in his own tongue as he dropped to his knees and shrugged off the wound. He readied his rifle to fire, only to see with his own eyes and in disbelief that the enemy were already aiming a second shot. Another volley rang out, once again with a fraction of the audible crack that muskets would make, and still with no cloud of powder smoke. Ferreira was hit again as a ball glanced his leg, and two more of his men were struck down.

Sporadic rifle fire from the Portuguese riflemen returned, and Craven was quick to join them. He directed his pistol in an ambitious and desperate hope of hitting anything as the others with him opened fire, too. They watched in horror as their attackers seemed to reload their peculiar rifles within seconds and prepared to fire again. Another group of twenty men rose up from ground further to the South and targeted Craven's force. A quiet ripple of a volley echoed out just as with the others, and Craven felt one ball skim off his greatcoat and another clip his calf. He watched in horror as their attackers once again prepared to fire, seemingly readying their weapons in a few seconds. They seemed to just manipulate the lock and keep firing without the need to put ammunition down the barrel nor use a ramrod.

"What devilry is this?" Paget cried out before he was struck in the shoulder and collapsed down.

Another volley rang out. Charlie was struck in the hand, and Moxy's shako was blown off as a ball sliced the top of his head open. They all scurried to find cover from the rocks and dried bushes around them, but the volleys kept coming with the same near silent release as if they were firing bows and not guns. Shots continued to whistle in all around them, and more were hit. Few managed to return fire and then struggle to reload whilst shot after shot was poured in against them. Craven looked around. More than half of them were wounded whilst some lay dead. They were all battered and bloody, and he could see there would be no victory there.

"We have to fall back," he said to himself in disappointment, "Fall back!"

He got to his feet and rushed to Paget's side.

"Go on!"

He helped Paget up and got another look upon the terrifying weapons that were brought against them. From a distance they looked like a typical rifle, but they continued to load and fire without pause and only seconds between their shots. He dragged Paget away as he continued to cry out for them all to fall back. More lead whizzed past them. Several found their mark as more struck the rocks around them. Finally, they made it over the crest of the hill and stopped to catch a breath. They were in a ruinous state and had left nine dead on the hillside whilst most of the survivors were badly mauled.

"Come on, we must not stop," gasped Craven.

They staggered down the hillside. Several of them needed help to walk, but they were relieved to see the rest of the Salfords advancing forward, which would protect them from any follow up from their mysterious attackers and their terrifying rapid fire smokeless rifles. Finally, they reached the bottom of the hill and began to gather their horses. Craven helped Paget up into the saddle.

"What was that? What were those awful weapons, Sir?"

"I have heard of such things, but never seen them," declared Ferreira.

"I've never seen or heard of such a thing," declared Vicenta who felt as powerless as the rest of them.

"I have heard them called the Windbüchse, the wind rifle," explained Ferreira.

"We'll discuss it later, let's go!"

Craven got onto his own horse before cautiously peering up towards the hill, half-expecting the enemy skirmishers to appear and rain down more fire upon them. He wasn't going to wait to find out as he led them on and back towards the security of the rest of the Salford Rifles. Although as he approached, he wondered what such an increase in numbers would even do against the sustained rapid fire of what they had just faced. It was one of the most terrifying experiences of his life. He had rarely ever felt so powerless and utterly at the mercy of the enemy. He was reminded of the weakness he felt against Bouchard in the darkest of days, but never had the battle been as one-sided as what they just experienced. He looked across to Ferreira as they rode on. Almost every one of them was covered in blood, either their own or their comrades who they had assisted. The expression on Ferreira's face told him everything, for he knew what they faced and was just as terrified.

CHAPTER 12

Screams rang out as Matthys went to work as the most capable surgeon amongst them. Paget was already seen to. With a ghostly expression on his face, he was sitting over a fallen tree and beside a fire that was the only relief they had. The sun was going down quickly, and there was a look of shock and bewilderment amongst them all, even those who had not fought against the so-called wind rifles. Matthys soon finished up with the help of Vicenta and several others and came to join them, his hands heavily stained with blood which he could not easily wash off.

"Well?" Craven asked.

"Eleven dead all told, four who must be sent back for care which I cannot give, including Ellis, and many more with wounds that will not heal for weeks or months."

"We don't have weeks or months." Craven shrugged off his own injuries, which were fortunate enough to be little more than flesh wounds, but more through luck than any other factor.

"Ellis?"

"His wounds are severe and potentially fatal. I have sent him and several others back to seek treatment."

"And will he live?"

"I cannot say. I really cannot."

Craven sighed, it being such awful news as his closest friends gathered about the fire. Amyn was the only one who did not look shell shocked, for nothing could compare to the horrific murder of the hundreds of his own people of which he was the only survivor. If anything, it seemed to bring some relief, that it was not just his kind who suffered so severely and unfairly.

"What happened there today?"

"The enemy set a trap and we walked right on in," replied Matthys.

"I can see that," seethed Craven.

"Wind rifles you said?" Paget asked of Ferreira.

All fell silent as they were eager to know about the seemingly impossible advanced weapons they'd faced, which appeared a technological marvel that none could even have imagined, let alone believe could exist.

"Girardoni rifles, I should think, and used by the Austrians."

"I have seen many rifles of all kind, but none like that. No powder and seemingly no time to reload," croaked Moxy.

"Indeed, the Girardoni and others like them do not use gunpowder to project the ball, but instead they use air."

"Go on," insisted Craven.

"These rifles use a container of compressed air to propel

the lead forward. If they are indeed the Girardoni, then it is in the butt. They do not need to be loaded with cartridge or ramrod, or anything put down the muzzle to load them, and each rifle carries a well of lead balls. Imagine not needing to put anything into your rifle to make it ready to fire again. All one must do is manipulate a lever and cock to fire a second, third, and fourth shot, and up to twenty all up."

Gasps were heard whilst others remained morbidly silent. It was a terrifying prospect that the enemy would have such devastating weapons when they did not.

"And after those twenty shots?" Moxy asked.

"Each man carries several tubes with which to refill the well of their rifle, and spare air chambers also so that they may go on firing with little delay."

"How do the French have this new invention?" Craven demanded to know.

"It is not new. It has been in service for many years in Austria, longer than any of us have worn a uniform, and longer than many here have even lived."

"Then why is this the first we are seeing of them?"

"The Girardoni is a true marvel of a weapon, and when it works as intended, it is like nothing any soldier has ever seen before, but therein lies the problem. It is a complex weapon, which is prone to several weaknesses, to which most armies would consider entirely unacceptable."

"Perhaps if they had been in the line of fire of these wind rifles, they might think otherwise," groaned Craven.

"Is this the work of Bouchard, Sir?" Paget asked.

Craven took a deep breath as he considered the possibility.

"It could well be."

"How can we fight this? The enemy set traps the way we have done so many times, but they beat us at our own game, and with far more effective weaponry," asked Ferreira.

"Moxy?" Craven asked.

"Those wind rifles, they are most formidable," he admitted.

"Weaknesses?"

"Range, even working at their best they cannot outshoot our rifles, not by a long shot," replied Ferreira.

"Which is why they used those American long rifles to draw us in?" Paget added.

"Those are almost as tall as a man," sighed Craven.

"But not nearly as effective at range as our weapons," replied Moxy.

Craven looked stunned as he waited for the Welshman to go on.

"The long rifle fires a small calibre ball at a great velocity as the powder burns for longer in that vastly long barrel. Less weight in ammunition and less lead used per shot, ideal for a frontiersman. You would not find a better weapon for hunting, but nonetheless it is still a small calibre and cannot reach the ranges of what we have."

"How far?"

"Two hundred yards, maybe a little more."

"Few amongst us can reliably hit anything over two hundred."

"Speak for yourself," jabbed Moxy.

"How far can you shoot and still hit a man?" Ferreira asked.

"Three hundred easily, four hundred in good weather, and

some say five or six hundred."

"And you can do that?"

"I'll outshoot any Frenchman with a long rifle, I promise you that," declared Moxy confidently.

"And once we have dealt with the long rifles, then what?" Matthys asked.

"We can't win a shooting match with those wind rifles," admitted Craven as he took out a map and studied it carefully.

"We could drive them onto the open plains and run them down?" Paget suggested.

"How many rounds a minute can those wind rifles shoot?" Craven asked Moxy.

"A full load I should think, easily."

"Twenty shots? You want to make a charge against twenty volleys?"

The young Lieutenant was mortified by the prospect, and he would never risk his beloved Augustus in such an ill-fated endeavour.

"No, we will not fight these weapons where they have the advantage."

"Then when?"

"At night, when none of us can see a damned thing."

"We have to find them first," replied Matthys.

"Tomorrow we will go looking and they will find us, and Moxy will get his chance."

"And then what?"

"Then, Mr Paget we will not fall into the same trap a second time."

They all took some relief in the fact that Craven had a plan. Their confidence had been badly shaken that day, and many of them showed the scars of the battle, but they soon settled in for the evening.

"How is the shoulder?" Craven asked Paget.

"It is sore, Sir, but in truth I feel quite fortunate. For my thick coat took the worst of the impact, and I do not believe those wind rifles strike with the same force as our own weapons."

"They did plenty enough," sighed Craven.

"Yes, Sir," agreed Paget as they both reflected on the frightful scenes, "Imagine if whole regiments were equipped with such terrors?"

"If they were truly so useful, we would see more of them."

"Then I pray they never reach such heights, or at least that if that day comes, it is us who has them in any quantity and not the enemy."

Craven groaned in agreement.

"If that day comes, I fear there will be no use for men like me. For what can a sword do against twenty shots a minute?"

"Then let us put an end to this war before such a day comes," agreed Paget.

"The last we spoke of it you thought we could not win, and you let Le Marchant's doom and gloom overcome you."

"I forgot myself, Sir, and I forgot what you taught me. One can never win a battle if he does not believe he can. I believe we can win this war, and to think otherwise would seal our fate."

Craven appreciated the sentiment, and yet he knew the General had a point, even if he would not admit it. But his smile was washed away as he looked to Matthys who looked particularly glum. The dried blood of his patients still filled the crevices of his hands and fingernails as he looked into the fire, lost in deep in thought.

"Excuse me." Craven left the Lieutenant's side and went about the fire to sit down beside the Sergeant, who did not even notice his arrival.

"Hard day today," admitted Craven.

But still Matthys seemed not to realise he was even being spoken to. Craven finally jabbed against his friend's arm. Matthys snapped out of his long gaze and jumped a little before recognising Craven.

"A hard day, I said."

"One of many," he sighed.

Craven knew there was a lot more on his mind than just the bloodthirsty day, for he had not been right for many days before it.

"You hounded Amyn today for doing precisely what was needed of him. He did his duty, but still you hounded him, why is that?"

"I have seen too much death and butchery. More than any man should ever have to see. In truth, I reached such a place years past, and still I carried on, but I do not know for how much longer I can take it."

"But why Amyn? Why aim all of your anger at him?"

"Because we brought that man here. We took a ruthless murderer out of a place where such behaviour is normal life. And we brought him here to kill men who should rightfully be our friends, and soon will be whenever this damned war comes to an end."

"The Portuguese brought me here, to kill fellow Christians, and to train them to kill them, too, so how am I any different? Answer me that."

"You are not, but that Moor is far easier to hate than a man I have followed for so many years." Matthys had sorrow and regret in his voice.

"Not one man here deserves to be hounded as you did. We each owe one another our lives many times over, and frankly, he owes us nothing. He could have boarded a ship and sailed a long way from this war a long time ago, but still he stays, and he fights, not because he likes killing. He stays for us, because we have given him a new family. He fights for the same reason you do."

"Then I have failed in my duties as a man, and I am sorry."

Craven laughed as he wrapped an arm about Matthys' shoulders.

"What is so funny?"

"That for once you are the one in the wrong," he continued to laugh.

Matthys thought about it for a moment before finally seeing the funny side and chuckling a little.

"Forgive me, for there is something I must do."

He got up and walked across to Amyn, who sat alone and silent, but looked up as Matthys approached and stopped, towering over him.

"Today I treated you unfairly, Amyn. For you are a good man, and I am a fool for not seeing it, and for that I am sorry," he declared sincerely.

"I am not a good man. I have known good men, and I know some still."

"Then you are a better man than most," added Matthys as he held out a hand in friendship.

Amyn rose up before him and took it.

"As are you," he declared.

Craven felt a warmth in his heart. For such a bleak day had dragged them all down to dreadful despair and melancholy, and already he could see they were healing. And finally, he could take some time to think for himself and not spend it in grief and misery. His thoughts soon turned to anger as he thought of his nemesis who was surely behind the events of the day.

"Bouchard?" whispered Craven, "I'll find you. Today, tomorrow, a year from now, I'll find you," he swore to himself.

* * *

"Will this work, Sir?" Paget asked as they buttoned up their coats over several layers and wrapped blankets and anything else they could find about their bodies.

"The ball that struck Ellis was small and did not penetrate deeply. Did you know the French cuirasses of their heavy cavalry can shrug off a musket ball at long-range? And a pistol ball far closer?"

"Yes, Sir, and indeed it is a wonder our own cavalrymen do not wear the same. Perhaps we should remark as such to General Le Marchant on our next meeting."

"That man would not ever don armour, for speed and agility are everything to him. But such armour can indeed stop a musket ball."

"But this is not armour," protested Paget at the thick layers they wore.

"When the Crusaders marched into the Holy Land, they

wore great shirts of chain mail, did they not?"

"Yes, they most certainly did." Paget was surprised at the apparent change of subject which he did not understand.

"But did you know it was not those links of metal that stopped the arrows of horse archers from killing the men who wore them?"

Paget shook his head.

"The rings of steel slowed the path of the arrow, but many of those rings broke on impact. It was the thick quilting beneath which stopped those arrows, and so it was not unusual to see an armoured man with a great many arrows sticking out from him, but with no wounds beneath."

"But we do not have metal rings over us," questioned Paget.

"No, but the great range at which we will be shot from with a small calibre rifle will reduce that velocity for us, and we now have the padding to do the rest."

Paget did not look confident.

"I do hope you are correct, Sir."

"You are welcome to go without."

But Paget shook his head, for he would rather have something than nothing.

They rode on through the cold conditions where the extra layers were a welcome barrier to the bitter weather. They rode throughout the morning and much of the afternoon without any sight of the enemy. They came to a halt at a crossroads to survey the ground all around them, but they had only stopped for a brief moment when something struck Paget. It felt as if he had been punched, but the thick quilting over his body had dampened the blow heavily. He looked down in amazement to see a small calibre rifle ball falling from his coat. The cracking sound of rifle fire soon echoed out having covered the distance.

"This is it, Moxy, get up here!" Craven roared. He retreated another twenty yards with the others as the Welshman dismounted and went forward. He lay down prone and put his shako down on the ground before him. Ferreira and three others laid down their rifles next to the Welshman so that he might fire without reloading. They backed away to give him space to calmly go about his business.

"Pretend to have been hit."

"Sir?" Paget asked.

"We do not want to spook them. If they aren't making progress here, they will move on."

Paget got off from his horse and lay down, as Matthys knelt over him pretending to help a wounded soldier.

"Dismount. I want a defensive perimeter, now!" Craven ordered.

The troops scattered as if getting to cover and firing positions, seemingly not knowing where they were being hit from. They gave the impression of being confused and defensive, the perfect mask for Moxy to go about his work. Craven took out his spyglass and used it from behind the cover of his horse's nape as he stood beside the animal. Moxy placed the muzzle rifle on his shako as a rest and brought it to full cock as he slowed his breathing.

They could see the powder smoke in the distance from the shot that had struck Paget, and just a moment later there was a flash of light as another was fired. The ball struck Ferreira and fell inertly to the ground, causing him to smile, and just a few seconds later Moxy pulled the trigger. The fine ground powder in the pan went up in a quick flash before the muzzle fired into life. Craven watched intensely as the attacker who had just shot at them watched to see the result of his shot, but instead was shot in the head and killed instantly.

"He does it again," smiled Craven. He then watched as the second Frenchman checked on his dead friend before continuing on to load his hugely long barrelled rifle and take aim for another shot. But Paget was ahead of him as he had simply taken up another of the rifles which lay beside him, and already had his finger on the trigger. Once again, he fired, and Craven watched as the man who had set the ambush was struck in the neck. He dropped his rifle, holding his bleeding wound as he vanished from view.

"Two for two!" Craven cried.

The Salfords cheered at his success as Matthys helped Paget back to his feet.

"You were right, Sir," declared Paget as he held the rifle ball in his hands that had bounced off of his thick clothing.

"What now?" Matthys asked.

"We make camp here!"

"Will the enemy not attack us, Sir?"

"Across open terrain when we have the range on them, I do not think so, Mr Paget," he smiled as Moxy reloaded his rifle in readiness.

"Then we wait, Sir?"

"For now."

Some of the men went out to forage for firewood and any feed they could find for the horses. It was not long before they had several fires raging and made themselves as comfortable as they could be.

"What then for tomorrow, Sir?" Paget warmed himself by the fire.

"Tomorrow? I mean to attack tonight."

"Tonight?" Paget asked in amazement. It was pitch-black away from their fires and freezing cold.

"Nobody can survive this night without a fire, can they?"

"No, Sir," admitted Paget as he imagined stepping away from the fires to go after the enemy.

"Then they will have fires of their own, and there is one weakness of those damned wind rifles they cannot overcome, the same as us."

"And what is that, Sir?"

"They cannot see in the dark," added Moxy.

Craven smiled in agreement as Paget finally realised the Major's strategy.

"You mean to turn this into a sword fight?" he smirked.

"You're damned right I do."

They waited a little longer until the visibility beyond the fires was entirely gone. Thirty of them slipped off into the night, and some of the dismounted men of the Salfords took their places so that anyone watching from afar would see the fires were well kept and attended, and not grow suspicious. Craven led his party on foot. For they could not risk the thunderous sound of horses alerting the enemy, nor could they see well enough to direct horses on such a black night.

They marched far to the North as they circled around any potential pickets which would have been set to watch out for them. It was a long and arduous journey, but the hard slog at least kept them warm in the freezing conditions. Eventually, they caught glimpse of two fires in the distance. They could not know who had set them, but in their guts, they knew it was the same force that had attacked them. Moxy used his tracking skills all the way and had no doubt.

Finally, after another hour they were closing in on the enemy and halted to survey the scene. Paget tapped Craven's arm and directed him to a glimmer of movement as he identified the sole picket. He swayed back and forth, stretching his limbs as he tried to stay warm and wait for his time beside the fire.

"Is it them, Sir?" Paget whispered.

"It is," declared Ferreira, as he could make out the unique Girardoni rifles propped up against trees near to the fire. To the untrained eye they looked little different to a Baker rifle, but behind the trigger was a large brass collar where the stock screwed on, containing the entire air reservoir for which they carried spares in leather pouches that also carried their unique speed loaders.

"Sir, another," whispered Paget as he spotted a second guard with his eagle eyes.

Craven signalled for Charlie and Joze to go forward, being the lightest and most agile of all of them. They put down their rifles and went forward with just blades and snuck through the night as quietly as could be.

"When this starts it will heat up awfully quick. We cannot let them deploy those rifles, do you hear?" demanded Craven of Ferreira.

"I know," he agreed.

"One shot from each man, and then we go in," added Craven.

Ferreira passed on the orders so that they were whispered to every man in turn. The riflemen took up prone positions and drew out their swords, placing them down on the ground ready to take up as they went forward. Craven watched intently but soon lost sight of the two who went forward and vanished into the darkness.

"Come on," he muttered to himself.

But they did not have to wait long. Charlie appeared seemingly out of nowhere and slit the throat of her target. She vanished down into the darkness as all eyes turned to the last target, waiting for Joze to do what must be done. Finally, they caught sight of him as he made his final approach, but they heard voices and noticed another Frenchman approaching to relieve the picket.

"He's going to be seen," gasped Paget.

"Prepare to fire," Craven whispered to Ferreira.

They were all ready now with muzzles on target and fingers on triggers. They did not wait for the order, but only for the first shot to break the peaceful scene and signal the volley. Joze kept moving forward, ready to pounce, but he hesitated as he saw the pickets switching over. He waited patiently as the two men chatted for a moment. Then the one who had been standing in the cold shivered and quickly ran off to warm himself by the fire. Joze took his chance and rushed at the newly arrived soldier who saw him at the last moment. Joze moved like lightning and placed his left hand over the man's mouth, driving his broad bladed dagger up into his body. The task was done, but a cry rang out in panic as the body of Charlie's victim was discovered. The first crack of a rifle echoed out as Moxy took his shot and felled the one who had found the body. A second later, a volley rippled out from the others as those about the fire were riddled with accurate rifle fire, and many were shot down where they sat.

"Now!" Craven ordered.

They rose up with swords in hand and charged towards the campfires. Charlie was well ahead of them and leapt out of the darkness onto one who had got his rifle primed and ready to fire. Charlie's sword slashed down at his lead arm and cleaved his hand off at the wrist before a second blow opened his throat. She went on without mercy.

Several of the enemy threw down their rifles or did not even try to reach for them, as they ran off into the night in some hope of saving their skins. Only three men got a shot off, and none had the time to load a second into the breech, despite the few seconds the job took with the ingenious design of the air powered rifle. Cold steel glimmered about the fire as blows rained in amongst the French soldiers. Some desperately attempted to use their rifles to defend themselves but to no avail. Craven's force struck them down with ease as they turned the tables on them, following the deadly ambush the day before.

Even Matthys did not shy away from the violent slaughter as he hacked against one and drove the point of his sword into another. It took less than a minute for the fight to be over, with Charlie, Birback, and Caffy vanishing into the night as they chased after those who had run, but there were no cheers of success this time. They had done what needed to be done, and their own losses weighed heavily on their minds.

"So, this is what all the fuss is about?" Craven picked up one of the remarkable Girardoni rifles, and Moxy took another.

"Incredible, are they not?" asked the Welshman.

"In fully working order, and the right hands I have never seen such a terrifying weapon," admitted Craven.

"Your orders, Sir?"

"Gather up three of these and the equipment bags they carry with them. We will retire to our own camp this night."

CHAPTER 13

Paget awoke in surprising comfort to find Charlie placing more logs on the fire beside him to keep him warm. The sun had been up for some time, and it had not caused him to stir. He was exhausted for having marched and fought through most of the night. He did not even get up and the only sign he had awoken was his eyes opening.

"How did you sleep?"

"Better than I expected to."

He wanted to stay under his blankets and warm in the crude but comfortable bed he had made for himself, but his sense of duty and pride got the better of him. He cast them off and got up. He looked around but could see no sign of Craven.

"Where is the Captain…I mean Major?"

"He left not long ago."

"To go where?"

"You will have to ask him on his return," she replied

bluntly.

Paget looked most put out.

"What have I done to anger you so?"

She said nothing as she poked at the fire with a stick.

"Please, tell me," Paget pleaded.

She finally huffed and looked back at him.

"I want to see you live."

"I do not want to die."

"But you may well do so if you do not take better care of yourself."

"It was you who was first in last night if I remember correctly."

"Because those were my orders, and that is what needed to be done. I worry for you, Berkeley, for I fear you try too hard to impress us all. You have nothing to prove, for you have proven it many times over."

But Paget did not look happy to hear it.

"Please don't ever ask me to stop being a man. I will not accept mediocrity. I want more from life, and I will do everything I have to for that end."

Charlie smiled as she knew he would never change, and she admired him for it, for it came from a well-meaning place.

"Then we go on to achieve great things together."

They looked upon each other with much love and compassion but could not reach out for one another. They could not be seen to be anything more than colleagues, and a precious few knew otherwise. They heard a rumbling of voices and looked over to see Craven approached on horseback with only Moxy by his side.

"Captain…I mean Major, Sir!" Paget cried as Craven leapt

from his horse, having given his mount a spirited ride on the frosty morning.

"Where have you been, Sir?"

Craven said nothing as he lifted a weapon from slung over his back and presented it out before the Lieutenant as a gift. It was one of the hugely long barrelled American long rifles with which they had been harassed the past two days.

"I cannot replace the rifle you lost in Lisbon, but perhaps this will do."

Paget was stunned by the gift and the realisation that it was the reason the Major had been gone. He did not know what to say, but Charlie smiled in appreciation, knowing what it would mean to him.

"Take it," insisted Craven.

He took the weapon. It had been freshly cleaned and oiled that morning and showed no signs of the dirt, powder residue, and frost for which was the state it must have been found in, having been left where its last user fell. It was huge in Paget's hands, reaching all the way to his nose when he dropped the butt down to the floor. Yet it was light in his hands, just as Moxy had said, it was a small calibre and with narrow furniture. It was a precise and delicate instrument compared to the large bore muskets and rifles he saw every day. It was in so many ways like a longer version of the treasured rifle his father had gifted him but refused to replace.

"She's as good as new, new flint, and I've pried the frizzen spring to ensure the powder stays in the pan and you get a good spark," insisted Moxy.

Paget did not know what to say, and whilst he looked appreciative of the Welsh sharpshooter, he soon turned his attention to Craven, who he knew must have been the driving force behind the mighty gift. It was the best gift anyone had ever given him. It had not been bought with money but sought out with love.

"I have always desired one, Sir, and now I will put it to good use as we march into Spain," he promised.

"Some men say a weapon is merely a tool of our trade, but we know better than that, don't we?"

"Yes, Sir."

"War might seem like a crude business to some, and for some indeed it is. But in fact, it is in precision where victory lies for many. Wellington will tell you that when he pores over maps and reports and lists, and whatever else keeps that man busy. For us here fighting at the front, it is the weapons in our hands and how we choose to use them. You are a rifleman, Paget, and you always have been."

"And yet the Army says an officer may not carry a musket or rifle, since long before you joined the service, Sir," smiled Paget.

"When have we ever done what the Army has told us to do? We make our own successes in our own way, and even Lord Wellington himself has begrudgingly learned to appreciate that fact. He placed you and I together to break us both, didn't you know that?"

Paget grumbled and shrugged as if he had some inclination but chose to ignore it.

"Wellington said a washed out rogue and an annoying young boy, neither of which he put much stock in. He imagined he might get rid of us both, not in battle, but that we might drive each other mad, and he might never have to deal with us again.

But against all odds, we did the opposite, did we not?"

"We did indeed," smiled Paget.

"Your father is a fool to not send a replacement rifle to you. Perhaps one day he will realise it, but somehow, I doubt that. But I do not care for his thoughts or anyone back in England, for they are not the ones out here fighting. Your father chose to be selfish, but you and me? We found a way around our differences, and both became stronger for it. Don't fret and wait for your father's love, not whilst you have better men all around you. This is where you belong, and if fate truly exists, then it is where you were always meant to be."

Tears came to Paget's eyes, and Matthys watched on in disbelief that Craven spoke so kindly and so openly, but it endeared him further to all who listened as they all gathered around to hear what the day had in store for them all.

"We have done what was asked of us. We have swept all French forces before us. The army makes their advance on the city now, and I will have all those on foot advance to join the siege lines. All those who are mounted will ride North with me and continue to do what we have done. We will drive the enemy from our path. I know you have all heard the rumours from Spain. Some say we march to failure and to face the whole French army. But I say this, we have broken the spirit of the French more than once, and we will do it again, for we will not be broken!"

Paget was the first to raise his newly acquired rifle into the air and cheer in support of the Major. Many others soon joined in.

"It is a new year, and with it comes new opportunities. Three times the French have driven into Portugal. I promised

Captain Ferreira and his countrymen there would not be a fourth. The time for retreat and stagnation is over. Remember Talavera, remember how we once advanced into Spain? Now we do it again, and this time we will do it right!"

More cheers rang out, and he waited for them to calm down.

"They say we Englishmen are pig-headed and stubborn. Well, let's show the French just how true that is. Let us show them what we are made of!"

A final cheer rang out as Craven turned back to all his officers and signalled them to go about their business. Even as the snow fell and the bitter winds swept over them, there was an excitement amongst the troops. They knew that finally the tables were being turned, for it was they who were going forward and taking ground. Yet they were also painfully aware that they had tried to take a fortified city from the French before. The failed attack on Badajoz was still fresh in many of their minds, but for now the momentum was with them, however fragile it might be. Craven quickly gathered up his things and was on his horse in no time. Paget was still fixated on his new rifle, marvelling at it as though it were the most beautiful thing he had ever seen.

"Come on, Mr Paget."

"Oh, yes, Sir." He slung it over his back, the stock almost touching the ground from where it hung. He climbed onto his horse as Moxy approached to give him something.

"You'll be needing these, Sir." Moxy handed over a shallow melting spoon for lead with a pourer on one side, and a musket ball mould which was remarkably petite, with which he could make the small calibre ammunition for his newly acquired rifle.

"Thank you."

"It is a mighty gift, for I should much like to have kept it myself," smiled Moxy.

"And yet you outshot its previous owner?"

"Different tools for different jobs. You will not find a better rifle for accurately shooting at medium distances."

"But not worth its salt at the longer ones? For I saw the balls bounce from my clothing and have no effect."

"Aye, but you can leave the long ranges to me, Sir. Soon the winter will be over and the coats put away."

"You would use this in battle?"

"Do not underestimate the long rifle. I might have exploited a weakness, but few men ever could."

Paget looked unsure.

"Is a pistol not fatal when used as intended?"

"Why, yes, it is."

"Then you have your answer. When the Americans used these rifles across the plains and frontiers against redcoats they played merry hell with our boys, and many a man lost his life. Some would say they are a symbol of the revolution."

"Then it would not please my father to know I now wield one," he smiled as he took great comfort in the fact.

"Move out!" Craven roared whilst many still struggled to gather their things, but those who would ride with him soon gathered on the trail and fell into line. It was Matthys who took up position beside Craven at the head of the column, but to Craven's surprise.

"That was a very kind thing you did, for Lieutenant Paget."

"I think we need more kindness in our lives, don't you?"

"Without a doubt, but you are the last man I would ever expect to hear say so."

"Then let me be your voice of reason for once and let us turn things entirely on their head."

"Oh?"

"Kindness can go a long way and it can buy things money cannot."

Matthys sighed as he knew where this was going.

"Our Mameluke friend has showed us kindness," declared Craven.

"And he has also done terrible things."

"Haven't we all?"

Matthys shrugged as he knew it were true.

They rode on throughout the day. It was not long before they could see French scouts, who ran upon sight of them. Again and again, they pressed the French, but none would engage. After the third time they had seen the enemy off they stopped to catch a breath.

"Will they not fight for the city, Sir?" Paget asked.

"Oh, they will certainly fight, but for the moment the odds lie in our favour, and the only thing the enemy have as advantage are the walls of that place. They would be foolish to fight us out here on open ground."

"Then why do we keep pursuing them, Sir, if they will not fight?"

"Because they are scouts, and they are here to gather information, and by denying them the ground we deny them that information."

They went on, and as they came over the next ridge, Paget gasped at his first glimpse of Ciudad Rodrigo. It was not the most formidable fortress in the land, being a second-rate fortress, but it was still an incredible and intimidating sight to know they would have to seize it from the enemy who were sure to put up a spirited defence.

"The French took this city by force, and we can surely do the same," insisted Paget.

"Marshal Ney was up against the Spanish, poorly trained and with low morale, but we face a far harder task against French regulars. They won't give it up lightly," admitted Craven.

"You truly believe this is the place that makes or breaks the war, Sir?"

"It has to be. If we cannot make progress this year, then we never will."

They watched as British and Portuguese forces approached. They spread out to occupy every local village and shelter they could find as they readied for the days and weeks ahead.

"Come on."

Craven led them towards the city as allied troops began to circle around and surround it, giving the impression they did not just mean to blockade the city but to assault it on multiple sides, though few believed they would. They approached the city and soon found a small house with a view of the city walls. It was in a poor state but still weatherproof and had clearly been occupied by the French until the last few days. A barn nearby would even keep their horses in remarkably good conditions compared to some of the awful conditions they had survived through.

"This will do nicely."

Craven stopped to look out at the city as the rest of them went inside. Only Hawkshaw and Paget came to join him and observe the enemy defences. The city of Ciudad Rodrigo was built on the North bank of the River Agueda, on an oval-shaped hill rising one hundred and fifty feet above the river. The city was surrounded by a thirty-foot medieval wall, with the additions of modern 18th Century fortifications built around it. Except along the river frontage, where the position of the old fortifications left no room for further defences to be constructed. To the Northwest of the city, a stream flowed along a valley, beyond which was a small ridge.

"That is the Little Teson," declared Paget.

Beyond the Little Teson arose another valley and brook towering over the former feature.

"And that is the Great Teson," added Craven.

Paget looked impressed that he had studied his maps also.

To the Northeast of the city were the suburbs in a low-lying area. Five convents stretched out around the Northern boundaries of the city, and it was hard to imagine how they could not feature in the defence of the formidable city. The Great Teson was higher than the city, and so the French had built a redoubt on the Southeastern corner of it called the San Francisco Redoubt, after the convent over which it looked.

"It will be no easy feat to overcome all of this," declared Hawkshaw.

The sorrow was clear to hear in his voice. He had lost the stomach for war and Craven did not decry him that. For he had achieved more and done more for all of them than most ever would, but he could sense that his time by their side was coming to an end, and a brutal siege could well be the final nail in that coffin.

"Our work is out here. We may leave the assault to other

men, for that is their work," declared Craven in the hope that he could save his brother from despair.

"Is it now our duty, Sir? Why would we not?" Paget asked.

"In a fight like that it is not the best shots or the best swordsmen who turn the tide, but a great many brave fools."

"Is that not what we are?"

"Leave it to the infantry. We have fought our war out here on the edges, but now it is the work of great formations of infantrymen to swarm into deadly breaches."

"You would let other men do this but not do it ourselves?" asked Paget in near contempt.

"We risk our lives nearly every day, but for many of those soldiers they sit comfortably in cantonments and wait for their moment to risk theirs. The assault of this city will be brutal and savage, but it is merely a concentration of what we face all year round."

Paget did not argue any further, though he did not look convinced.

"Come on, let us get warm."

Craven handed the reins of his horse to Joze and went inside. A fire was already being set alight in a welcome sight, and for a little while it was easy to forget they were within sight of a mighty French fortress. They made themselves as comfortable as they could be. Craven lamented the lack of wine, but in truth he was exhausted, and the rest of them were in no better state as they each began to drop off to a deep sleep, of which they all needed.

CHAPTER 14

Craven got up to stretch and found it was remarkably cool. The fire had long gone out, and there was little sunlight to warm the house. He pulled on the greatcoat he had used as a second blanket and stepped outside, imagining it to be warmer out there. He carried his sword in hand but looked to be in a ragged state, and yet was met by the most unusual scene of Lord Wellington riding casually toward him. For a moment he imagined it was a mirage and all in his mind. He raked his hand in front of his eyes as if to shoo it away, but as they rode nearer, he could see the General was in fact real. He rode with only a handful of his staff and no protection at all. Wellington appeared calm and jolly as though he were enjoying a morning hunt back in England, but his eyes were always on the great walled city as he rode up to Craven.

"Ah, Major Craven!" They stopped near him.

"Sir," he replied cautiously, as if expecting to be given an arduous task to conduct.

"Craven, this Lieutenant Colonel Fletcher, commanding the engineers."

"The man who built the Lines?" Craven asked, referring to the mighty defensive lines at Torres Vedras which had saved the Anglo Portuguese army and stalled Marshal Masséna's vast force, ultimately breaking the back of that army.

"I certainly played my part, and so did you," replied Fletcher.

There was a nod in appreciation between the two men, for they could appreciate one another's devotion to a single field and the success each had achieved in it.

"What do you say, Captain, sorry, Major," went on Wellington.

"About what, Sir?"

"We ride around the fortifications as we make our plans, and so how would you do it?"

"The same way you, the Colonel here, and any capable Frenchman would," replied Craven honestly.

"Go on," smiled Wellington.

"The Great Teson is the key. It is the perfect position to place heavy guns and equally as useful in defence should we attack elsewhere. It must be taken with all haste if we are to progress. Then take the Little Teson and bring the walls down before it."

"You have some experience of this sort of work, Major?" Fletcher asked.

"I know how to spot a weakness and how to exploit it," admitted Craven.

Wellington laughed.

"Perhaps I have found another who can do your job, Colonel!" he roared at Fletcher.

Fletcher took it in good humour as Wellington's staff laughed along.

"Dirty business it will be here," admitted the General, which brought the mood down.

"We will do what must be done," Craven answered.

"Will you, Major? Will you?"

"What would you have of us, Sir?" Paget rushed enthusiastically to join them.

Craven shook his head, knowing the Lieutenant would drop them in to deep water as he was always overly enthusiastic.

"The men of the Salfords have proven themselves quite the fighters. I can use men like that. Be ready tomorrow, Major, for when the sun goes down the fighting will begin."

"Where, Sir?"

"At the Great Teson," smiled Wellington, confirming Craven was correct. But in truth, nobody was fooled by the General assessing the walled city from all sides, as nobody but a fool would approach from any angle but the heights of the Great Teson.

"Have a good day, gentlemen," added Wellington before riding on.

"We will get our chance, Sir!" Paget yelled excitedly.

Craven would be furious if he wasn't certain they would have been volunteered whether Paget was involved or not.

"How can the General ride about the perimeter without an escort, Sir?"

"How could anyone catch him? He rides a healthy corn-fed horse, and the French can barely muster a few sorry looking creatures. How would they catch him?"

But Paget watched in concern as the General and his staff rode away.

"If I were you, I would worry more about your own skin," added Craven.

Paget thought about it for a moment before he noticed Charlie was staring at him, judging him in deep concern.

"I am not sure I know how, Sir. I only know how to go forward straight at something."

The Major smiled and nodded in agreement as it reminded him of himself.

"I am not sure worrying about death will delay it any," added Paget.

"No, but we need not speed it up either."

"What now, Sir?"

"Like most of the army, we wait."

The day past slowly as they welcomed the luxury of the old house and chatted amongst themselves, glad to be out of the saddle and the cold weather. Even so, the thought of the assault hung over them like a dark cloud on the horizon, but they did their utmost to pretend it did not exist, as soldiers were so good at doing. They played games and relived memories as they made as merry as they could be, glad to be in in the warm as others went to work building breastworks and other fortifications around the city.

It was gruelling work in the sleet and freezing rains, but a lot worse lay ahead, and they all knew it. The next afternoon they watched as troops swarmed about the perimeter of the city in manoeuvres surely intended as much to blockade the city and intimidate its defenders, as it was to conceal the evening's operation. Craven led a party of only those equipped with rifles to the North to join in the operation Wellington had alluded to. He had less than thirty riflemen by his side, which seemed a most modest number in the shadow of the mighty fortress, their presence not attracting any attention as they casually walk in plain sight of the walls.

"Do we assault this night, Sir?" Paget asked.

"Yes, I am certain of it," replied Craven as they looked at the fortifications ahead. The Little Teson lay just two hundred yards from the walls of the city, whilst the Great Teson was almost seven hundred yards from the same walls and rose up high above the smaller elevation. The Great Teson which was their target this evening was four yards taller than the main walls of the city, a fact which would put the defenders at a significant disadvantage should Wellington be able to take the heights and allow him to fire directly down and into the city's defences.

"But without first besieging them?"

"Time is not on our side."

"No, Sir?"

"If Marmont hears of this, he will march to the relief of the city."

"Is it not dangerous to assault without first besieging?"

"Everything we do here will be dangerous, and you remember it," insisted Craven.

They were losing light quickly now as they continued to advance, and it was not long before those in the city would lose sight of them entirely as they marched on through the bitter night. Craven brought them to a standstill. They were in open ground for all to see, but with so little visibility in the darkness there was no chance of them being seen this night.

"What do we wait for, Sir?"

"Whatever Wellington has ordered."

"And he has not shared that with you?" Paget sounded worried.

"We are not here to conduct a mission, Lieutenant. We are a contingency."

They waited another hour, and finally, they could see the glimmer of movement as hundreds of troops approached. They had abandoned all equipment that would dangle and crash together and give off the familiar sound of marching infantry. They moved cautiously but quietly and with intent, ladders in hand. More than four hundred of the Light Division advanced under the secrecy of the dark night. Paget could hardly believe his eyes. For to make an assault after the siege had not even begun seemed preposterous, but there was no doubt it would give them the element of surprise. The French had prepared for a long siege and not such a brazen assault. Even from a distance they could see the enthusiasm on the faces of the ten companies of Light Infantrymen as they moved on the French position. All of the boredom and frustrations of the winter were melted away as if the spring had finally come, and they moved with a great excitement to finally get at the enemy. Caçadores were amongst the British companies who approached to make the assault.

"And so what do we do, Sir?"

"Make sure you have that long rifle ready; you are going to need it."

Craven led them forward, following the assault party as they approached the defences. They were just a few hundred yards from the French positions, close enough that a good marksman might hit a man on the walls. They could make out the silhouette of several French soldiers on the walls, and evidently, they could see the advancing troops in return as they cried out in panic, trying to alert their comrades to the remarkable surprise attack.

"Charge!" roared one of the British officers.

The Light Division companies surged forward with ladders in hand, moving with immense urgency as the first shots rang out from the defenders.

"Come on!"

Craven led the way forward before taking a knee in range. He knew all of his riflemen could hit the mark, even if he could not.

"Fire at will!"

Moxy got off the first shot, but it struck part of the defences, and Paget fired next. He hit the man Moxy had missed in the arm, causing him to fall back from view.

"You're losing it Moxy!" Craven shouted, causing laughter to ring out as more fire was poured on the French.

Only fifty-five Frenchmen defended the Great Teson, which seemed like nothing at all, but amongst such strong fortifications it would commonly be enough to hold off an army for some time, but the assault this evening was not conducted in the typical way. Wellington had become famous as a cautious commander, and no one could have imagined him making such a brazen assault without any prior preparations and bombardment.

That was the beauty of it, and they could all see it. It was a surprise attack which genuinely had the element of surprise. Shots rang out back and forth as those skirmishing from a distance tried to keep French heads down as the men of the

Light Division placed their ladders up against the walls. The first two were thrown back down as musket fire rained down on the assaulting red and brown coats, but skirmishers peppered the walls; including those under Craven's command and a party of sappers carrying fascines threw them into a ditch beside a short palisade. They formed a bridge from which many of the Light Division men rushed across and jumped into the ditch. They readily scrambled up onto the parapet and came into bayonet contact with the enemy without need of ladders.

The suppressive fire was so effective against the defences that the French troops threw shells and grenades randomly over the walls, not risking being in the sights of the skirmishers who would shoot them down if they showed their faces or tried to use their muskets. Yet as Craven watched, he was quickly becoming impatient. He could take no part in the shooting gallery. All he had was his pistol, and he would be wary of hitting their own troops even if he did have a rifle. He watched as their troops began to climb the ladders. It was clear the French had so few to face them, having been prepared to hold off a bombardment, but not a direct assault. An explosion rang out at the doorway to the rear of the defences, giving an easy route in for those who had encircled the fort.

"Come on!" Craven drew out his sword and ran forward to join in the attack.

There was little fire coming back at them. The French troops on the walls hurried to reload their muskets, were wounded, or too busy fleeing back toward the city. Musket and rifle fire lit up the dark sky as war cries rang out and the terrified Frenchmen tried to resist the onslaught. Being outnumbered almost ten to one, their resolve was already wavering as the

British and Portuguese troops climbed the ladders, and the first men climbed up over the defences and to battle the enemy on the parapets.

It all hung in the balance. For once the attackers gained a foothold, the battle was almost certainly over. Craven reached the base of a ladder and almost ran up it as he leapt onto the wall with sword in hand, ready to do some damage. He noticed a Frenchman finishing to reload and ran at him. The French soldier hurried himself and left the ramrod in his musket as he quickly raised the weapon to fire one desperate shot, ramrod and all. Craven cut up at the muzzle, sending it high into the air just as the powder flashed and the ramrod was shot out high into the darkness. The Major took hold of the weapon and lifted his sword point to strike.

"Sir! Sir they are running!"

Paget got up onto the wall. British and Portuguese troops swarmed across the defences from in front and behind, encircling the enemy as the last of the Frenchmen ran for their lives. They leapt from the walls whilst some of the wounded remained and others surrendered, accepting their fate. Craven looked back to the man he had effectively disarmed as he could do nothing with his musket now it was held firmly in place.

"Surrender?" he asked the Frenchman, knowing that most soldiers in the war would get his meaning.

The soldier looked relieved as he released the grip of his weapon to Craven, who tossed it aside. Many of the troops around them had surrendered, with the last of them fleeing and running for the protection of the city. The night had fallen silent as the musket and rifle fire had come to an end. The assault had been a massive success with only a few casualties amongst the

Anglo Portuguese, with many seemingly in shock and surprise that it had ended so quickly and so successfully.

"It's all over," remarked Paget, but his jubilation turned to horror and disgust as several of the Caçadores who had taken part in the assault now abused the prisoners they had taken, stripping them naked and robbing and beating them.

"Sir?"

Craven did not like it, but he could understand their actions.

"You saw what the French did to Portugal, can you blame them?"

Paget looked deeply uncomfortable as he tried to put himself in their shoes.

"Leave them be. It is not our business."

It had taken only twenty minutes to overcome the great heights which overlooked the fortress city. The Salfords moved forward to the walls to look out towards the city where they could see lanterns lighting up the grand fortification. In the ground between they could see glimmers of movement as the Frenchmen who had fled rushed back for the protection of the great walls. The vantage point was only a few yards taller than the walls of Ciudad Rodrigo. To many men that would not have seemed of note, but to any man who had taken part in a siege, they knew precisely how valuable it was. The Light Division companies celebrated their success. They cheered, and several even fired their muskets into the air in celebration.

"This bodes well," declared Paget as he looked out towards the city beside Craven.

The Major nodded in agreement, though he did want to be too optimistic yet. He was remembering Badajoz and prayed they would not have a repeat.

The wounded were seen to, and positions were taken to ensure there was no counter assault. Although few believed it possible. The French Garrison had a great quantity of supplies, but few soldiers. Yet those who had fled had just as soon reached the city when the cannons opened fire and erupted with great violence in the quiet of the night as the Great Teson was bombarded relentlessly.

"Get down!" Craven roared.

They took shelter in the very French defences they had just assaulted, glad of the fact the Royal Artillery had not gotten a chance to flatten them. Paget huddled into a corner near Craven, and they felt the defences shake as cannonballs struck them.

"They do not give it up easily."

"But they have given it up. There is nothing but spite in this bombardment."

Paget calmed down as he realised it were true. The Great Teson was theirs and nobody could take it from them now, nothing short of a relieving army could do so. The bombardment was ruthless and seemed to go on unreasonably long, inflicting some casualties, but nothing which would make it worth conducting. Eventually, they had all come to accept it and relaxed. They could not predict where and when the French shells would land, even as more of the valiant soldiers who had assaulted the fortification become injured as they took shelter in the very same defences. The heavy bombardment went on and on until finally, the guns fell silent as if they had either accepted they could do no good, or that they had taught the enemy a lesson and had stopped for the night.

"We are going to do it this time, aren't we, Sir?"

"We know it, and the enemy knows it."

"And then it is a sure thing?"

Craven looked away and took a deep breath of the cool air before looking to reply. He found Paget had fallen asleep where he sat with his sword resting across his lap. He smiled before nodding in agreement.

"A sure thing?"

He chuckled to himself, remembering the number of times he had said the same thing as a terribly awful gambler with such awful luck. He rested back and realised how exhausted he himself was and finally closed his eyes, falling off to sleep almost as quickly as the Lieutenant had.

CHAPTER 15

Paget felt himself being rocked awake as if it were a dream but awoke to find it was Charlie who shook him.

"What...what...what is it?" he demanded as he rubbed his eyes and clenched his cold fists to find his knuckles click in the frosty morning. His ice-cold blade was frozen to the touch as he sheathed it and got to his feet. Charlie pointed to a position along the wall where Major Spring was deep in conversation with Major Craven. Paget coughed to clear his throat and adjust his uniform to appear as smart as he could whilst he rushed to their side.

"Excuse me, Sir," he declared in apology.

"Spare me your excuses, Lieutenant. I heard you were there climbing the ladders last night," replied Spring.

"Yes, Sir," replied Paget modestly.

"Then you're a damned fool, but at least you are our damned fool."

"Thank you, Sir."

Orders are to change the troops in position here every twenty-four hours, so that no man spends more than a day at the front suffering through this."

"Is it optional, Sir?"

"No, it is not."

"Then I am sorry to say I will not comply, not unless Major Craven orders it," he declared as Craven joined them.

"Did you hear that, Craven. Mr Paget refused orders," he declared in a light and amused tone.

"I've heard troops withdrawing to the rear must ford ice-cold water across the Agueda. Up to their shoulders they say, with their pouches up on their knapsacks and holding one another like a chain so they are not forced down current and drowned. If they don't freeze to death first, and then spend much of their time on duty in freezing wet clothes, is that true, Major?"

Paget shivered at even the prospect of it as Spring begrudgingly agreed.

"I think I'll stay in range of French guns thank you," Craven said firmly.

They watched as engineers began work on gun batteries whilst hundreds of infantrymen who had been brought up to assist them worked to install fascines and other breastworks above the rock-hard freezing ground. But as they worked, the French cannonballs flew and struck with remarkable accuracy. Just as soon any British position had been established, and construction began to install the guns required for the siege, the French opened fire and smashed them. And from the vantage point they now held called the Great Teson, they could see the situation was the same all around the city where Wellington's army slogged to emplace themselves. The so-called San Francisco redoubt named after the convent it overlooked to the North of the city, and which edged the Great Teson where they were currently standing, was the greatest target of enemy fire. It was not directed at the point they were standing, but just fifty yards away where gun emplacements were attempting to be established. The French fire was unrelenting.

"Damn fine gunnery." Major Spring watched in horror as two men were killed and another one carried away from the latest French strike. It was a remarkable scene. For they themselves were in the line of fire and yet were not a target. The French only fired upon the gun positions, for which they knew to be the only current threat.

"If you will not leave, then I have a task for you," declared Spring.

"Yes, Sir?" Paget asked excitedly.

"The French make continuous attempts to carry news to Marshal Marmont of this investment. Remember that time is not on our side. This cannot degrade into a long siege, for that is why we marched through an icy hell to be here so early in the year. If Marshal Marmont learns of our attack, he will march to relieve this place and there will be hell to pay. I am sure you now understand the importance of victory here. We cannot be driven back into Portugal again. Marmont must not learn of what we are doing here until it is too late for him to stop it."

"What can we do?" Craven asked.

"We have scouts on the lookout for anyone who tries to escape the city, but I would have you join them, for little ever slips through your fingers. This is a job you are most well suited to and is of the utmost importance."

"You want us to hunt messenger boys?"

"Yes, I do."

"And what should we do with them, Sir?"

"Shoot them down, take prisoners, I don't care. All that matters is that no communication gets through to Marmont. You will deliver any papers you discover directly to me or burn them if you cannot."

"And if Marmont already knows about all of this?"

"Then pray he does not, Major, and we work on the assumption he does not. Everything must progress just as we need it to."

"And when does that ever happen?"

"Perhaps we will have a stroke of luck this time. The taking of the Great Teson was a stroke of luck, was it not?"

"Luck played no part in it."

"Indeed, but we caught the French by surprise, and we are now several days ahead of the schedule they would have expected us to keep. I imagine they thought it to be a prolonged affair, for us to be battling back and forth for this redoubt of theirs for a week or two, if not more. Momentum is in our favour, and we must keep pressing forward. You know what you have to do, gentlemen. Hunt the enemy, and do not let a word go West. The affair hangs over all our shoulders, and if we stay true and do all that is required of us, we will have this city and spit in the face of Napoleon. This is the advance into Spain, and we will not be stopped. Remember that."

"Yes, Sir."

Craven signalled for his small party to withdraw from the Great Teson and find their mounts. In truth, it was a relief to no longer be standing still in the cold and in the face of French artillery fire which plagued all the British and Portuguese troops who struggled on.

"Is this really needed, Sir, or are we merely being sent away?" Paget sounded worried that he might be losing out.

"If you are concerned about missing the assault, don't be. For it will not be tomorrow, nor the day after, but weeks from now."

"I know, Sir," groaned Paget.

"I don't know if the Major sends us away as an act of kindness or not, but he is right about one thing, this is what we are suited to. It is just like old times," smiled Craven as he led a small handful of irregular troops to operate on the fringe.

They could hear the roar of cannons at their backs as they went on, glad to be away from it all. They returned to the house they had used for shelter to find it had been occupied by a full company of Light infantrymen, but they were falling out to go about their duties, leaving a roaring fire inside. Craven's party shuffled inside and gathered about the log fire, shivering as they warmed themselves, still feeling cold all the way to their bones. Now Paget had gotten a hint of warmth he didn't want to move.

"Why must war be fought in this bitter weather?" he pondered.

"To gain surprise over the enemy," declared Hawkshaw.

Paget nodded along as he knew it to be true, but it didn't make it any easier.

"Many men and women must suffer to work through days like this in peacetime," replied Moxy. It was not so surprising to him, for he had always had to work for a living, whereas Paget had lived a lavish and lazy life until arriving in Portugal.

"Yes, I imagine so. I remember hunting on cold mornings

like this with my father, and I always marvelled at the bleak faces of those who were not along for the hunt. Now I understand why, for we rode for fun and then returned to the warmth of a fire whenever we desired."

"It's nothing to feel shame for. You cannot change how and where you were born, as does any poor fellow," added Hawkshaw.

"No, but I might have treated men differently had I understood it. I lived a very good life, and yet still I had my gripes. It is hard to imagine how hard it must have been for many."

"None of that matters now. None of us is where we imagined we would be all those years ago. Frankly, I didn't think I would live this long," admitted Craven.

"No, Sir? Really?"

"All they that take the sword shall perish with the sword," stated Hawkshaw.

"And you believe that?" Paget asked Craven.

"Not entirely, for many a man has lived through many battles and lived to a good old age, but there is plenty of truth to it. For there are not many old warriors, are there?"

"I have spent much time with family and friends who lived through the war in America and elsewhere," replied Paget.

"And how many more were dead and buried?"

Paget shrugged as Craven looked to Hawkshaw with curiosity after his recital of the Gospel.

"Do you believe it?"

Hawkshaw shrugged as if in agreement.

"And yet you yourself live by the sword. You dedicated your life to the sword so that you could kill me. If you believe in those words, then you accepted it would seal your fate also?"

"I didn't care about my life, only ending yours. I was a young fool, were you not the same once?"

"We are still," smiled Craven, causing them all to chuckle as they rubbed their hands together and finally began to feel themselves again.

"Can we take this city, Sir?"

Before he answered Paget, he noticed Hawkshaw take particular interest. It was clear to Craven that so much was at stake, as Hawkshaw's resolve could be broken by failure, and it was a sentiment felt throughout the army. The remnants of positivity and enthusiasm would only hold firm so long as they kept going forward and achieving successes. It was a lot to ask for after the toing and froing of the previous years. The truth was Craven did not know, but he stuck by his own advice and chose to believe they could as they all waited on his response.

"Of course, we can. We have been through a lot, but just remember the French have been through it, too. Are you tougher than them?"

"Certainly," replied Paget as if feeling he needed to defend all his countrymen and not just his own honour.

"Major Spring gave us a job to do, so let us get it done."

Craven knew a ride out beyond the siege lines would do them all a lot of good, despite the fact it could be dangerous, but that was nothing new to any of them. They mounted up and headed out with Moxy and Joze well ahead, and Craven and Paget leading the small column. Seeing Joze filling in for Ellis brought the wounded former officer to the forefront of all of their minds.

"Do you think he will live? Ellis?" Paget asked.

"We can only hope, but there is nothing more we can do for him now, except ensure we are victorious, so that he need not fret or be moved away from an advancing French army."

Paget took it seriously. That was an excellent additional motivator as he looked at the great fortified city and the thousands of Anglo Portuguese troops encircling it.

"But how can any messenger get past our lines?"

"Encircling a city is no easy task, and a few men might get in or out without being noticed, especially at night. How do you think I got into Almeida during the siege?"

Paget huffed in frustration.

"War is such a complex affair, Sir."

Craven chuckled in response.

"Why is that funny, Sir?"

"How could it not be complex? Organising tens of thousands of soldiers, and supplies and food, and wrangling the enemy. A fight between two swordsmen is a complex affair, but all of this is something else entirely."

Paget shrugged in agreement as they rode out into open country. It was a quiet place. Those who worked the land had either fled into the safety of the city or scattered out across the rest of the country, far from the roar of the cannonball. They rode on for many hours, circling back and forth as they screened the terrain for any sign of the enemy. Finally, they spotted horsemen approaching, but did not pause as they could see Timmerman at the head of the column. The two forces came together as friends.

"Major Craven it is, for that is what I hear?" Timmerman smirked.

"Indeed," Craven responded and who still felt awkward

with it.

"Do you still hunt Bouchard?" Paget asked him.

"Invariably, but he is a tricky fellow," grumbled Timmerman.

"He certainly is."

"I heard you and your boys were shot up with some particularly brutal weapons?"

"Where did you hear that?" Craven sounded astonished he would know.

"Come on, Craven, I am more than just an angry drunk."

"We did, and we lost some good men."

"The work of Bouchard?"

"I imagine so. That bastard hangs about us like the plague."

"And yet you had the chance to kill him? You could have finished him without a fight," Timmerman remarked on the time Craven had found Bouchard close to death and unable to resist.

"I am a fighter, not an executioner."

"I don't think the Frenchman sees the distinction."

"But we do," declared Paget firmly.

"Then you fight this war your way, and I will do it mine, but if I find Bouchard deep in sleep, I will not hesitate to slit his throat," declared Timmerman proudly and with no shame.

Paget was disgusted by the notion, but Craven began to wonder if he were right. And yet as he looked to his brother, he knew he could not sink to such lows, or risk losing all those who followed him. Even so, as he gazed upon Timmerman, he realised he could be quite the potent weapon in their arsenal.

"I can't make you do anything, but you do what you have

to do."

"What are you doing out here?" Paget asked.

"The same as you, looking for the enemy."

"And if you find them?"

Timmerman merely smirked, as they all knew he would not be taking prisoners, and yet this version of the Major was far more desirable than the wild card he used to be. Paget still hated him for what he was, but was simultaneously glad that he no longer hunted them, and instead he hunted the French.

"So, will you go for the breach to be the hero once again?" Timmerman asked Craven.

"Only a fool would go anywhere near it."

"Yes, and I would not have you die such a needless death," replied Timmerman endearingly as he gotten quite comfortable with his old nemesis, just as Hawkshaw had with Timmerman.

"We should be on our way, for we should not be all gathered together," declared Craven.

"Good luck to you," replied Timmerman, surprising them all at his good faith before riding on.

"I didn't ever believe that man could change, and yet here we are," said Paget.

"None of us are what we once were," Craven said.

They rode on back and forth but found no sign of the enemy all day and settled in for the night beside a fire. They sent out constant patrols to work through the night as they searched for any Frenchmen daring enough to try and slip by in the night.

Craven was awoken to take his turn. The first rays of light were on the horizon, a time he would never choose to be up and about as he groaned but got up to do his duty. Paget and Charlie joined him as they mounted up and rode on to make their sweeps of the land. Three other parties did the same. Campfires had been kept alight all night, and that had saved them from freezing to death, but it was still brutally cold. Craven could hear ice and frost cracking on his blanket and greatcoat as he moved. He rode on, hoping the sun would bring them less bitter conditions.

"How could any man escape the city and survive in this, Sir?" Paget asked.

"When one's life depends on it, a man may do the seemingly impossible, and you know it."

They swept back and forth, occasionally catching glimpses of other parties doing the same, but eventually, the sun was up. They had found nothing, and they rode on back to their camp to warm themselves by the fires once more. They approached Moxy who was on duty and stopped.

"Anything?" Craven asked.

"Nothing."

Craven groaned as he knew the enemy must have tried, and it concerned him they had not seen any evidence of it.

"Craven!" Birback was pointing to a slope far to the West. A man scurried up a muddy slope wearing no uniform. They knew it had to be a Frenchman out of the city, for no other person would be out there alone. Craven turned his horse about and rode after the man with Paget and Charlie following suit, having already been in the saddle. They raced towards their target, but he had a major head start and very soon vanished over a ridge as they lost sight of him.

"He cannot get away!"

Craven angrily spurred his horse on to go faster, but the conditions were a mix of slippery frost and mud, which did not allow any great turn of speed. They raced on and on and briefly caught a glimpse of their target. He went up and over another ridge in the distance before vanishing once more.

"Find him!" Craven shouted angrily.

Paget had got well ahead of the two others as Augustus carried him on with a supreme turn of speed without needing to be urged to do so, seemingly knowing the importance of his task. On and on they raced as if all their lives depended on it, when in fact they knew many more than just theirs was at stake. None had taken Major Spring's assessment to heart more than Paget, who firmly believed if word got out from Ciudad Rodrigo to Marshal Marmont it could spell disaster for not just the siege but the entire war. Paget tore over one embankment with the others left far in his wake, and he caught sight of their target once more.

"Over there!" he cried as he led the way in the pursuit.

He could not help but be reminded of those cold hunting days with his father, and he remembered the excitement he felt as it was the same as he felt now, but there was one thing which was very different. Back in those hunting days he had treated it all like a game, with no consequences. He remembered it as a carefree time, but now he went on as if everything were on the line, and failure would let down Wellington himself. He came up over another ridge, and finally, the man was in sight. Paget drew out his pistol and rode on, but musket fire erupted ahead, and he abruptly brought Augustus to a halt so as to not lead him into the path of danger.

Craven and Charlie rode up beside him just in time to see several more shots hit the fleeing Frenchman. He was cut down and filled with lead as if by firing squad. Moments later, a dozen Spanish guerrillas came out from some bushes to check on their victim. They wore a mix of clothing, some of Spanish regular army uniforms, but mixed with British and French equipment as well as civilian items. They looked so ragged it was hard to know for certain if they were a militia or merely Bandidos, but nobody questioned it, so long as they fought against the French.

The poor Frenchman was already dead before he had even struck the ground. Paget sighed in disappointment. He'd have rather captured the man alive, and he didn't want to see the tenacious Frenchman dead after such a brave escape attempt. It made him feel remarkably fragile, as he realised that could have been him so many times. The ambush with the wind rifles could just as easily have seen him riddled with as much lead and left him dead on the hillside.

"Come on."

Craven rode on towards the body. The Spanish fighters looked a little skittish as they approached, which was understandable as their tunics were over the cover of greatcoats of mixed manufacture. Craven unbuttoned his coat and pulled one side back to reveal his uniform.

"Good morning!" Craven cried.

But it was soon evident that they spoke no English at all, as Craven watched one of the Spaniards loot the body in search of anything useful. There was a satchel hanging over his body, which was the exact sort one might carry written orders or despatches.

"Tell them we want the bag," ordered Craven to Paget.

The Lieutenant struggled and stuttered as he tried to find his words. It was evident his grasp of Spanish was little better than Craven's, but a response soon came in a flurry of words. The only one Craven needed to understand was 'no,' and that made him angry. He climbed down from his horse to claim the satchel himself, yet as he approached, he found a number of muskets directed at him. The Spaniards angrily defended what they rightfully saw as theirs, seeing as they had killed the Frenchman on their own soil.

"Sir, I would be careful," insisted Paget.

Craven sighed in frustration, as it was not a situation he knew well how to deal with. He was not one with his words, and he did not even know how to speak their language. Nor did he want to draw weapons and escalate things further with men who were their allies, or at least the enemies of their enemies.

"We need that bag," insisted Craven as he growled towards Paget.

Another rider approached and went past Paget and even Craven, not showing any care for the muskets directed towards Craven. It was Vicenta. She shouted angrily at the men before leaping from her horse. She walked right past the muzzles of their muskets, pushed one aside, and straight up to the man who had taken the satchel from the body of the French soldier. She took it from him without a word as the Spaniards were frozen almost in fear. She took the case to Craven and thrust it into his hands.

"What did you say to them?" Paget asked.

"Learn our language and you will know," she snapped.

The standoff was cooled as the muskets were lowered and the Spaniards argued no further. Craven was astonished but merely glad it was resolved as he looked down at the bloodstained satchel.

"We must know if he had any other documents on him." Craven looked at the body and realised how easily information could be spread if they missed anything.

Vicenta approached the body and shooed her countrymen away as she checked the body herself, handling it no differently than a rabbit she had shot for food. She was as accustomed to death and war as any of them, and that shocked the men who had shot him down.

"There is nothing."

Craven looked to the armed men, suspicious of them, but also thankful they had been there when they were needed.

"Give them my thanks, and the thanks of Lord Wellington, for their service is greatly appreciated."

"They do not serve you or Wellington."

"But thank them, nonetheless. Without men like them, we would be in this war all alone and long defeated, I think."

Craven got back into the saddle and rode on to be out of the sight of the Spaniards before stopping to look inside the satchel. The papers were simple and short, and despite knowing little of French, he could tell it was exactly what he expected.

"A note to Marshal Marmont, Sir?" Paget asked.

"No doubt, or to any Frenchman. It will not be long until they hear of our work here," lamented Craven.

"But how, Sir? How if we stop any word getting out?"

"Something this big cannot be kept under wraps forever. The great guns rage to hear for miles all around."

"Then our work is pointless, is it not?"

"Far from it. Every extra day we can slow the news from reaching the enemy gives our lads one step up on a chance of victory."

CHAPTER 16

Craven held a steaming cup of tea in both hands. He watched from afar as British soldiers dug into the hard ground, creating an increasingly elaborate line of trenches. It was backbreaking work and made all the worse by accurate artillery fire which continually harassed those at work every day. They had retired to the house to rest for a little time as others took their turn, though Craven imagined Timmerman would still be out there. He was sadistic enough to suffer through the conditions just to not miss any chance at enemy stragglers.

"Poor bastards," declared Hawkshaw.

They had all seen a siege before but were used to the defences being built above ground, but the French artillerymen were highly skilled and were devils in their shooting. A new gun emplacement had just been completed on the Great Teson, only to be smashed and rendered unusable within an hour of finishing. The scene dragged morale down further as the troops slogged away with seemingly little progress. The jubilation following the taking of the Great Teson had faded after several days without any noticeable progress and mounting casualties. It felt as though they had been besieging Ciudad Rodrigo for weeks or months, and not the few days it had really been. Major Spring approached on horseback, causing Craven to sigh as he expected them to be criticised for taking some rest, but he was looking remarkably cheerful.

"What can I do for you, Major?"

"Nothing at all."

But Craven looked at him suspiciously.

"The papers you brought back were everything you thought they were. Damn fine work."

"Thank the guerrillas, for they shot the messenger dead."

"You are sure of that?"

"That man had enough lead put in him to keep him down for good," insisted Craven, knowing no man could survive such a brutal shooting.

"Yes, the Spanish people have proven quite the thorn in Napoleon's side. It is fair to say that they kill far more of the French than our army could ever manage."

"And what would you have us do?"

"What you are already doing. Buy us time, as much time as you can, but you are not alone in this task."

"Indeed, we crossed paths with Major Timmerman out there."

"Is he not one of you now?"

Craven groaned as that was in some ways true. They had welcomed him into the Salford Rifles, and yet it had never been official, and he had gone on to go about the war in his own way.

"You should be relieved. Before you left Lisbon, you were a wanted man. Many an officer wanted to see you dead."

"And because of him."

"I seem to remember it was rather more because of Captain Hawkshaw."

Craven's brother shied away in shame. They all knew it were true, but none of them were saints, and so they did not press salt into the wound any further.

"Just when it seems you are finished, Craven, you get another lease of life and your career."

"Career?" Craven had never thought of it that way.

"How many years have you been a soldier?"

"Many."

"Do a job long enough, and it is who you are. How many people know the name James Craven because of your prize fighter vs your exploits here in Portugal and Spain as a soldier?"

Craven smiled as it was a curious development. The idea of being a career soldier was something he had always laughed about, and yet he could see now that it was his path.

"How is it out there?" he asked, watching the French guns.

"The enemy certainly aren't making it easy. Just as you can see, as quickly as we build anything, the French guns blow it to bits. Our engineers work to build gun positions on the Little Teson, and as soon as they are complete, we might bring up the guns there to breach the walls, but it is proving a hard task."

Craven could see that with his own eyes, but he knew there was nothing they could do. There was nothing anyone could do but slog on in the face of relentless cannon fire.

"They will not give this city up easily."

"No, they will not."

"How long until the guns can be taken onto the Little Teson, Sir?" Paget asked.

"Honestly, it seems like we are not even close. If we could work without the harassment of the enemy, we might accomplish the task quickly enough, but they do harass us at every turn."

"We will get back out there." Craven knew that was the one thing they could do, ensuring the besieging army had as much time as possible to get the job done right.

They went on to conduct their sweeps of the area, but it was an uneventful day and an arduous task, the sound of cannon fire in the distance a constant reminder of how easy they had it compared to many. They soon set up fires so that they could take turns in the bitter cold and be ready for another freezing night. Craven once more took his turn on duty in the early hours before the sun had come up, and again he was joined by Charlie and Paget, but there was no such excitement this time as they swept the area.

"Sir?"

"What is it?" Craven groaned, expecting a complicated question of which it was too early, and he was too tired to give any serious consideration.

"What will Wellington do if we cannot secure the little Teson, Sir?"

"I wish I knew."

They rode on for another hour before hearing the thunderous galloping of horses from the West. Craven snatched his pistol from its holster, in readiness for whatever was coming their way, but it was Timmerman who came storming into view with a great urgency. He drew up beside them, his horse panting heavily from a hard ride.

"Marmont knows!" Timmerman shouted.

"You are sure?" Craven pressed.

"Certain, Marmont is on the warpath!"

"Wellington must know immediately," Paget added.

"My horse is shot," replied Timmerman.

"I'll go," Paget immediately volunteered.

But Craven knew it was too important to not go himself.

"No, get the Salfords back to the house and have them prepared and ready for anything."

"We do not leave a presence here?"

"The secret is out now. Our work here is done."

Craven turned back towards the city and launched into a gallop. He did not want to be the bearer of bad news. He could already imagine how furious Wellington would be, but he would be even angrier if he heard the news later than need be. He rode hard, and to his surprise he could see the General himself riding about the edge of the city. He galloped up to the party with the same sense of urgency Timmerman had arrived to deliver the bad news to him.

"Marmont, Sir, he marches against us!"

Wellington took a deep breath, adjusting himself in the saddle as he thought it over. He looked to the great walls of the city and the convents the French still held, and then to the two Tesons which were still a contentious area battled over in gunnery duels.

"Come with me."

He rode on towards the Great Teson where he could get the best view of the city and siege works. He dismounted and climbed up to the same position where Craven had slept several nights before. Still the French guns fired periodically on every position where the British worked to build emplacements, as well as all that had been completed. He leaned out over a wall with Craven by his side as his staff stayed well back and Major Spring climbed up to join them.

"So Marmont marches to Ciudad Rodrigo?" Wellington pondered.

"I fear Craven is correct," added Spring, clearly having heard reports which appeared to confirm the news.

Wellington looked at the Little Teson and the struggles which still went on to build a second parallel and more gun emplacements from where the artillery might bombard the defences. If they could ever be completed, considering the relentless French opposition. The ground all around the Little and Great Tesons was heavily scarred from days of cannon fire.

"A great army marches on us, and yet here we are facing what, two or three thousand French troops behind those walls?" Wellington demanded angrily.

"I am sure the French said the same when they were stopped before the Lines," replied Spring.

"Time is not on our side, no, no it is not. I need solutions, gentlemen. I need answers," confessed Wellington.

But nobody said a word as the strategy was the General's role.

"Get Fletcher up here," he ordered as he called for the commanding engineer.

The orders were quickly passed on as they waited in hope that he might have some solutions for them.

"Well, Craven, what would you do?"

Craven grimaced as he peered around at the intimidating

sight. He had no idea how to overcome a well defended fortress, but his attention was soon drawn to the Convent of Santa Cruz overlooking the Little Teson which was still in French hands.

"We cannot assault the city, so maybe we worry about what we can take instead of what we can't?" He directed Wellington's attention to the convent.

Wellington appeared relieved to hear some plan rather than nothing. He gazed upon the convent with a furious anger as the French held on to it defiantly, even firing down against the Little Teson from their position there.

"How many men do you think would it take?"

"Three hundred rifles," replied Craven confidently, demanding the very best to get the job done.

"I want it, and I want it tonight."

Craven nodded in agreement.

"The French are moving quickly, and so shall we," insisted Wellington just as Fletcher approached with another of his engineers.

"Yes, Sir?"

"What we feared has come, time is no longer on our side," said Wellington.

Fletcher sighed as he leaned out to assess for himself and could see the bloody struggle for the Little Teson still ongoing.

"We don't need it. We don't need the guns down there," he insisted.

Wellington looked suspicious, but Fletcher went on.

"Put the big guns here on the Great Teson, and I promise you we will make those breaches. We don't need guns on the Little Teson."

"You are sure?"

Fletcher looked to his staff officer beside him.

"And you are?" Craven asked.

"This is Brigade Major John Thomas Jones," replied Fletcher.

"It can be done," assured Jones.

"I am certain it can," added Fletcher.

Wellington looked to Spring and Craven as if to wonder if he was being told what he wanted to hear, but they all had faith in the most senior engineer. But he looked out to the trenches ahead as shells burst around and one direct hit landing amongst the men sheltering there.

"Get it done," he growled.

Other shells landed amongst the earthworks and exploded like mines, blowing away hours of work as earthworks erupted into the air.

"If you want me to deploy the guns, the convent there will be a problem," said Fletcher as he looked to Santa Cruz.

Wellington looked to Craven in agreement.

"Let the Germans have a crack at it," declared General Campbell from behind them.

Wellington looked curious, as he had come to rely on the resilient and dependable troops.

"Let me send Lowe," added Campbell.

"The KGL? Yes, they should get the job done," Craven agreed.

"Observe them, Craven, I want it dealt with," declared Wellington.

Craven could see the convent was in a ruinous state, having been battered badly in the 1810 siege. Breaches had been hastily filled with wood, and yet it was still a defensive position which should not be taken lightly.

"I want the walls breached at the first opportunity," growled Craven.

"Yes, Sir, it will be done," insisted Fletcher.

Little happened throughout the rest of the day, or at least little in plain view for the French to see, as preparations were made secretly for that night. Craven crept through the darkness to a place where he could see the Convent of Santa Cruz, and also the three hundred troops of the King's German Legion and the 60th Rifles which supported them. The subdued uniform colours of both units assisted in concealing them under the night sky. For a moment nobody moved as they readied themselves for the final run across open ground. They knew that once they began, they would be at the mercy of the gun batteries of the city until their work was done, whether they succeeded or not. The Captain leading the assault force knelt down beside Craven.

"Captain Laroche de Stackenfels," he declared as he introduced himself.

"Major Craven."

"I know," he replied in his thick German accent.

"The future of this siege is in your hands, Captain. We must take this position if we are to breach the walls of the city and make an assault. Good luck, Captain."

Craven took out a pocket watch to check the time before looking to the West just as a number of torches appeared, lighting up several dozen British troops moving with great speed and intent. It did not take long for the French guns to open fire on them.

"Now, go!" Craven ordered.

The German Captain signalled for his men to go forward

as he darted out into the night. They covered as much ground as they could whilst the French were busy dealing with the diversion that had been set.

"Will this work, Sir?" Paget scrambled up beside him.

"We can only hope. Did you get them?"

"Here." Birback handed Craven a large pioneer's axe and kept one for himself.

"What are you going to do with those, Sir?"

"What they were built for," he replied as he ran out into the darkness in pursuit of the German troops. It was an easy trail for follow as they went straight for the convent. It was clear to see silhouetted against the night sky, with several torches lit for the defenders who were on duty. Cannon fire roared, and soon enough the first shell landed amongst the Germans, killing one and wounding two more.

"They've seen us, Sir!"

"Thank you, Lieutenant, I might not have noticed!" Craven yelled sarcastically.

They scrambled on as shot and rounds struck the ground around them, but the troops were at a near sprinting pace as they hurried to reach their target and outpace the shots of the French artillery. Explosions rang out, and screams followed as many of the German troops fell down wounded. Paget looked down at them as if he wanted to stop and give aid, but he knew they must not.

Craven had caught up with the front line of German troops as they reached a wooden palisade that had been built around the convent. Cannon fire continued to rain down on their position as dozens of the Germans now lay wounded. Craven and Birback rushed forward with their large two-handed axes and began to chop in perfect time at several of the stakes. They struck one after another in rapid succession until one split and the other looked to be giving way.

"Give me some room!" Birback jumped onto the damaged stakes, and they snapped under his weight, sending him tumbling through just as he had gone through the windows of the French occupied house several weeks before.

Craven could not even get through the breach as the Germans swarmed in, and cries of panic rang out from the French inside. Many fled for their lives, leaving everything behind, even their weapons. Finally, he shoved his way through and drew out his sword expecting a fight, but there was no resistance. Several surrendered whilst most had fled, leaping over the walls and fleeing just as many had done during the attack on the Great Teson. A cry of success rang out, and both sides soon knew who possessed the convent as Craven looked out across the battlefield. They could see down into the parallel trench lines which were manned by the poor infantry around the clock.

"Poor devils." Paget looked down upon them huddling in place where they had to stay for twenty-four hours on duty.

"Someone has to do it," admitted Craven.

"Can it be done, Sir? Can the walls be breached?"

"If Colonel Fletcher says it can be done, it can be done."

"You have that much faith in him, Sir?"

"I have faith in his abilities. If you want to win a sword fight, you come and talk with me, but you want to take a castle, you speak to Colonel Fletcher."

"Then soon the guns will fire and see if the Colonel is right, won't they, Sir?"

Craven agreed as he looked at the formidable defences and hoped he was right to put his faith in the engineer who had not let them down yet in this war.

CHAPTER 17

Craven awoke to feel a shivering chill in the air, and his eyes shot open as he imagined what it must be like for those manning the trenches. They had been at Rodrigo for just one week. A modest period for a siege, and yet it felt far longer. Fatigue was setting in for them all, made all the worse by the unrelenting weather conditions for which the French did not suffer, as they took shelter in the well-equipped and comfortable fortified city. Many garrisons had been starved out throughout history, but it required time, and Wellington's advance in the winter was both a genius tactical move and also torture for those who had to conduct it, and that torture was taking a horrible toll that was more evident every day. It was as if the roles had been reversed, as it was the besieged French troops who had time on their side and the resources to wait out their opponents. Every day was a chore as they got up and wondered if they were making any progress at all.

They watched on from afar as the work went on in the same way it had for days. The British and Portuguese troops kept digging and working to build better defences to protect themselves and the guns whilst the French hit them with withering cannon fire at will. It was 11am when Craven watched the 4th Division approach the second parallel, the one closest to the city walls, and relieve those who had manned it for the gruelling twenty-four hours before. Yet the fresh troops were a long way off the position when the exhausted men of the 1st Division began to pour out of the trenches, not in the proportionate and staggered method required by general orders, but they emptied out all at once. Nobody thought anything of it until the first Frenchmen appeared from the city as they sallied out to attack the defences when they were at their weakest. The French had timed it perfectly, having monitored the troop movements as one division relieved another over the previous days.

"This doesn't look good," declared Hawkshaw.

"Gather the horses," ordered Craven.

"What is happening, Sir?" Paget asked.

"Just fetch out horses!" Craven cried angrily.

Paget looked put out but did as he was ordered and ran sheepishly away. Hawkshaw watched with an open mouth in astonishment as five hundred French infantry poured out from the gates of the city. They rushed towards the second parallel that had just been vacated, leaving only sappers, gunners, and engineers to defend the positions with few weapons to resist the enemy and protect the earthworks and cannons now positioned there.

"They are going to spike the guns! Come on!"

Craven shrugged off his greatcoat and let it fall to the ground as he ran on to fetch his sword, all he had with which to fight. Paget came out of the stables with both of their horses as the others readied their mounts as quickly as they could. Craven galloped on without giving any commands, but they could all see what was happening from their vantage point. Paget soon caught up with Craven. The Lieutenant was far better equipped, with his pistol in the saddle holster and his long rifle dangling from his back.

"How can they dare to do this, Sir?" Paget said in disbelief. He knew how much they outnumbered the enemy, and it seemed preposterous to him that they would march out to fight in open ground.

"They mean to undo the day's work!" Craven shouted back at him.

"Why? What difference could it make?"

"Enough to delay an assault a few days and let Marmont march to oppose us!"

It was now dawning on Paget that such a small error and perfect timing by the French could put an end to their hopes of taking the city, and therefore the war. He never believed so few men in so short a time could make such a difference, but now it was playing out before his eyes. The urgency of supporting those still in the trenches became a matter of more than life and death, but success and failure for the whole war. It spurred him on to ride harder as now he truly knew what it meant if they were to lose too much.

The French infantry did not march in line or column but merely darted across the open ground as a lightning raiding force. Soon enough they were at the second parallel and causing chaos. Royal Artillery gunners tried to fend them off with their broad short swords and a handful of muskets between them, as those digging were forced to use their shovels for protection. The French tipped gabion baskets back into the trenches, emptying them and undoing much of the previous night's digging. It was complete chaos as the French troops ran amok, ripping apart the results of days of back breaking labour in any way that they could. The second parallel was already abandoned, and it seemed as though the French would not be stopped as they pressed on for the first, where they would be able to disable a great many guns.

Craven galloped onto the scene but had to stop well short. The ground was treacherous where days of shells and digging had created a pockmarked landscape of dips and troughs. He drew his sword and raced forward as an engineer officer cried out to rally a ragtag punch of labourers and gunners to the parapet and fend off the next assault. Craven rushed to the defences as the engineer was throwing out muskets. It was Major Jones himself, and he tossed one of the muskets at Craven, not caring for his rank.

"Fire at will, fire at will!" he kept crying, urging the stragglers to put as much lead into the air and towards the French as possible.

Craven sheathed his sword and took the weapon. He pulled it to full cock and fired. He could not tell if he hit anything. It was complete chaos, but he quickly reached down for a cartridge box and continued to load. Paget rested his enormously long rifle on the parapet beside him and took careful aim. He fired and shot down a French sergeant with ease.

"Keep shooting!" Jones cried angrily.

Craven's closest friends rushed to his side, including Ferreira and some of his Caçadores. The combined weight of the withering fire was starting to take its toll. The French stopped advancing and took cover in the second parallel to return fire and continue to destroy the work which had been done there. Craven had fired his third shot when cries rang out as the relieving division approached.

"Let's see them off!" Jones climbed out onto the open ground and swung his sword about enthusiastically, "Who is with me!"

He charged towards the enemy to reclaim the ground they had lost. Craven let go of the musket that had been thrust into his hands and leapt over the parapet to draw his sword and run after the brave engineer who fought like a lion to protect what was theirs. Soldiers with a mix of red, brown, and blue jackets stormed on as an angry mob, wielding swords, muskets with bayonets, muskets wielded as clubs, and even some with shovels in hand.

They advanced rapidly with the relieving division in support. A great war cry rang out as they made their advance. Several shots rang out from the French, but in no time at all they were on top of the enemy and jumping into the filthy trench to do battle. Many of the French troops climbed out and ran as eagerly as they had advanced. For it was a terrifying counter charge, but Craven hacked at the legs of one man as he tried to climb out of the position. He dragged him back into the mud where Birback slammed the butt of his musket into the man's face.

Caffy leapt in also and swung his hefty cavalry sabre to cleave one man at the neck. He smashed another in the face with the butt of the rifle he held in his other hand. All along the line it was complete chaos as the French tried to flee, and few fought back. Cheers rang out from the troops that had taken back the second parallel, but the position was a mess. They could see the French troops fleeing back towards the city. They had made off with a great many of the tools and supplies they had found there.

"The buggers have taken our damned shovels," wept Jones.

"Have you not got more?" Craven asked.

"We never have enough of anything. Not enough tools, not enough powder, not enough ammunition, not enough time," he lamented.

But his melancholy soon passed as he looked back and realised it could have been so much worse. The significant French force could well have progressed far further and done even more damage.

"I thank you."

Craven shrugged.

"There are many men and many officers involved in this affair, but they did not come to our aid, and you did," he added.

"My boys will take any chance for a fight."

"Don't be so modest, Major. You got us out of a tight spot."

"Then tell me honestly, can we blow those damn breaches?"

"Yes, we can, and we will, and you, when the breach is made, will you follow us through it?"

Craven smiled, for Jones was a very well-spoken gentleman who would never have given him a moment's notice in everyday life. They were of a similar age, but Jones held himself like a man of great standing, and yet now in they were standing in the same mud together he was as friendly as if they were members of the same elite and exclusive boys club.

"If there is a fight to be had, I'll be there."

He turned back to see Paget's eyes glow at the prospect.

"Not a word," joked Craven as the troops of the relieving division swarmed in to take up their positions and ensure both parallels were now safe from any other opportunistic attacks. Craven recovered his horse and was glad to leave the scene as the French guns opened fire once again.

"That is it, Sir?" Paget asked in disappointment.

"It is not our job to man these positions," he replied as he led them away.

"But you said you would be there to go through the breach, Sir?"

"That will not be today, nor tomorrow."

He led them back to the relative safety of the house that had provided them with a better quality of life than most of the troops and even many of the officers. They watched from afar as they knew it was about to begin. They could see long lines of mule and bullock convoys carrying supplies at all hours of the day across the fifty miles of perilous roads between their supply lines in Portugal and back. They were stretched thin, and everybody knew it.

But late in the afternoon they watched as the gun crews of the heavy guns prepared to begin the bombardment that the engineers had promised would get the job done. The guns were not even visible to their eyes. They were lowered into trenches with recoil reducing ramps and double height gabion baskets before them. Earthen mounds piled up as glacis slope protection, with embrasures or gun holes closing off all sight and access to the guns from the front to the enemy when they were not firing.

It was a remarkable feat of engineering and manpower and went a long way to protect the gunners. But still the French played merry hell with the gun emplacements, as for all the protection they were not invulnerable. Yet those embrasures were being opened, and everyone knew what that would mean. The French guns were unrelenting and targeted the gun emplacements even as they were being prepared, killing several of the men whose dangerous duty it was to reveal the guns.

The twenty-seven heavy guns thundered in one great roar, a salvo far louder and intimidating than any they had heard before, and the troops all across the lines cheered as the shells smashed into their targets.

"That is curious." Paget was one of the few not celebrating the opening salvo, as most of the guns were aimed at the Northwest corner of the walls where the French had breached the walls when taking the city from the Spanish in 1810. The remaining were fired at the San Francisco convent.

"Enlighten us, Mr Paget," smiled Craven.

"Well, Sir, the convention is to target the initial fire at the enemy's guns to destroy or dismount as many as possible, but Wellington has had most of the guns work to breach the defences, why I wonder?"

"Because a whole French army of fifty thousand or more men is on their way to stop us," added Ferreira.

"That's right. If we are not inside those walls within a week, then it's all over," Craven stated clearly and openly for all to hear, as he wanted them to understand the gravity of their situation. This was not just another battle, but the result of which would decide the future of the entire continent.

"But we do not attempt to silence their guns, Sir?"

"There is no time, only one thing matters now."

They watched as the great bombardment went on for a full hour until finally daylight began to fade away, and they were forced to give up until the next day. The Salfords had set up a large fire well in front of the house so that they may all gather about it and keep a keen eye on the fortress. It meant they could be observed by the French guns, but that was the same fear they all lived throughout the day, and so it did not seem to matter. The guns were plenty busy enough dealing with the siege works before them.

Well after the sun had gone down, they heard explosions echo out and then musket fire off in the distance as a night skirmish erupted.

"The convent, Sir, San Francisco," said Paget as he had memorised the city well.

They watched musket fire light up the sky as a battle raged over the fortified convent, but it was over in a short time, and cheers rang out which spread throughout the siege lines, signalling the victorious capture of the place.

The next day was bitterly cold but dry and clear, and so the bombardment could continue in full. Craven looked out to trenches the French had damaged the day before. A workforce of the infantry had rebuilt and strengthened them more than they were before, as an engineer directed the men to place sandbags atop one of the batteries. He was in plain view of the enemy as a French cannon ball cut him in two. It was such a common sight that few men said anything and barely reacted, but soon after a terrible bombardment followed in a ferocious attack on the British gun emplacements. It was an awful thing to watch as it was so incredibly destructive, but still the British guns kept their focus on bringing down the walls. Simultaneously, riflemen in pits built ahead of the second parallel targeted the French gunners to do what they could to hinder them; even when it brought the wrath of the French cannon down upon them with grape shot. Paget could see it all and finally understood how awful it was, just as Craven said it would be.

"I wish it can be over soon, Sir, for no man should be subjected to this," he whispered, not wanting to show weakness to the rest of the regiment. Craven agreed but said nothing.

The days went on in much the same manner, but heavy fog was increasingly becoming a problem, halting the guns for hours and even whole days at a time. Paget looked to be despairing more and more every day as he watched the dreadful gears of war turn, where in a siege they were bare for all to see more than any other time. The fog at least gave time for the work parties to improve the defences, but it also lost the army valuable time as they waited with dread for Marmont and his great army to arrive any day.

"Why do they not surrender, Sir?" Paget asked as they watched the fog clear again and bombardment and counter artillery fire commence once more.

"Because they only need to wait out a little longer and we are finished," replied Craven solemnly.

Day after day the bombardment went on back and forth to horrific effect. Many of the British and Portuguese guns were struck and destroyed by French cannon. Some had their magazines blow, causing horrendous casualties to the men working on and around them. Paget was growing sick of seeing the tragic story unfold before his eyes whilst he felt powerless. But on the eleventh day of the siege, and under sustained salvos, the whole Western face of the city's walls came tumbling down in an almighty avalanche. It was so loud it drowned out all of the jubilant celebration which followed for a minute.

Anticipation was building now the breaches in the city's walls were there for all to see. And after the brutal hammering they had received outside the walls, the troops were eager to get their chance at the enemy. Yet the guns thundered on all day as they improved the two breaches to be sure of giving the infantry the best chance of a successful assault. Also, to divide the small French force of defenders across multiple positions, rather than be able to concentrate all they had in one position. Craven turned back to address the Salfords, knowing the time had come.

"There it is! What we have been waiting for. The city is ripe for taking, and I intend to take it!"

A cheer rang out as a troop of horsemen approached with Timmerman at their front. He dismounted and approached Craven, who looked wary but said nothing.

"I hear Craven himself intends to storm the breach?" Timmerman laughed, "Well, I should very much like to see it, and I can hardly watch from the sidelines. We are with you!"

The Salfords celebrated. They knew how formidable the Major was, and he was just the kind of savage fighter they needed in such a savage contest.

Craven accepted his offer, for he recognised it for what it was, but he soon turned back to his own troops who looked both eager and nervous.

"We will not lead the assault. Nor will I ask any man to do what I will not, but that city will be ours by any and all means necessary. A great French army approaches to relieve this place, and if we fail to take it, then all of this was for nothing. Not just this siege, but every battle which we have fought and every man we have lost. This is the moment where we either lose this war, or we prove to the French that they cannot win. What would you have? Would you have us give it all away?"

"No!" they roared.

"Then come with me and let us show the enemy what it means to be a Salford!"

They erupted with excitement as Craven turned to Hawkshaw.

"Have them formed and ready to fight but stay in sight."

"Where are you going?"

"Just do it. Paget, Ferreira, you're with me."

Craven headed for the trenches and Timmerman followed on beside them. They soon found Picton's 3rd Division was taking over from the weary and exhausted troops who had been there from the night before. The guns continued to rage, but it was three other men who Craven quickly recognised and headed for. He could see Wellington personally making his way along the second parallel with Colonel Fletcher for a close look at the work of the guns, so they could decide whether an assault could be made. There was much back and forth between them, and Craven could tell why. The slopes to the breaches had not been broken down as much as would be ideal. That would present additional unenviable challenges for those that would assault it. It would be an arduous and difficult scramble, with the French having a far superior defensive position from which to resist any attack. The lesser breach looked especially tough with a very steep climb.

Several of Wellington's staff tried to keep Craven away, but the General gestured for him to be allowed through.

"Colonel Fletcher tells me you were there to assist his man to resist the French infantry and save our positions, is that true?"

"I aided Major Jones, but he had it in order, Sir."

"Major, one thing I am very certain of is that if a situation requires the intervention of you and your bunch of ruffians, then it was not in order."

"Yes, Sir," Craven smiled back at him.

"Well? You can see with your own eyes the same as the rest of us. We have two breaches. How would you do this?"

Everyone was silent as Craven studied everything that was before him, and he seemed to blank out into a daze as he sometimes did when he was fighting.

"Don't go for the main breach straight away."

"And why is that?" Wellington asked as if knowing but wanting him to explain why.

"It is the best angle of attack, but we should draw the enemy away so that it is as weak as it can be. Launch a feint, a diversion, not just one, but two."

Timmerman chuckled and nodded along in agreement. He could see Craven analysing the fortress as though it were a swordsman, as he calculated how he could strike where he wanted with ease by approaching with a deception or two.

"Two feints, you say?" Wellington queried.

"The French have few troops, but they will be forced to respond wherever an attack is made, so why only attack in one place? We have the men to attack in a third location and further rob the enemy of their strength. Cause chaos for the enemy with a flurry of feints, and then strike home there when they are protecting all other targets."

"Do you think it can be done, Craven?" Wellington looked at the steep glacis of the breaches.

"You ask me, Sir, when you have experts in this field beside you?"

"I ask you, Major, because I know I will get an honest opinion, and not the one that any man thinks I want to hear, or has that changed?"

"If Major Craven recommends it, then I stand by him," Timmerman declared.

Wellington was silent as he looked at Craven's old enemy, amazed that they were even standing within a sword's reach of one another and not fighting.

"Like England and Spain who were once the most bitter of enemies, you two gentlemen, if either of you can be called as such, now fight together. I must admit it gives me some hope, as we hold together this army of men from a dozen nations."

The cannons continued to roar in the distance, as well as musket and rifle fire whilst sharpshooters went to work, but it was a fraction of the devastating fire of the previous weeks. Wellington turned back to the city to get another look for himself before nodding along as he muttered to himself. He took out a piece of paper from within his coat and a pencil as he began to take some notes.

"Sir?" Craven asked as he did not know what to do with himself.

"Craven, this is what we have been waiting for. We knew Rodrigo must be taken quickly, and we knew Marmont would march on us if he caught wind of what we were doing here. And so of course we go in, this evening, from three directions."

Craven was much amused by the prospect of his tactics being used by a man many considered to be a military genius.

"Ready your men, Craven. Tonight, we take this damned city."

CHAPTER 18

The sun had long gone down, and the evening chills were a familiar experience for them all, but something was very different about this night, and they all felt it. There was a dread that swelled in all of their bellies, no matter how brave they imagined they were, or anyone told them they were. Craven and the men of his Salfords waited behind the cover of one of the convents, which provided cover from the enemy on the still and clear night. The scenes were calm, but they knew it was the calm before the storm as the Light Division formed ahead of them, ready to storm the lesser breach. Craven was shaking his head.

"What is it?" Matthys asked.

"On no grounds would I ever have been here in the thick of it, how did it come to this?" he whispered.

"Paget would never have forgiven you if he missed it," smiled Matthys.

They tried to make light of it, but the fear was very real for them all. The troops around them were all volunteers to make the assault, a horrifically dangerous task, and only a little less dangerous than the forlorn hope themselves, the tiny party which were to be the first into the breaches and almost certain death.

"They say it's best to be on the storming party, to be put out of pain." Paget knelt down beside them, trying to calm his nerves and those around him.

It was true that many said that. For to be struck early before the worst of the barbaric action was underway, and perhaps the first to receive medical treatment, might be beneficial. But Craven shook his head, knowing that was merely a thing men told themselves and one another to soften the blow and make a most awful thing more palatable. Yet he would not share those reservations with Paget and break his spirit.

General 'Black Bob' Crauford paced back and forth ahead, as he was to lead the assault of the lesser breach personally. He certainly lifted the morale of those around him. Black Bob was both loved and loathed. He was a strict disciplinarian with a terrible temper so severe he would curse out his fellow officers, but for all that, he was brave and steadfast and had the love of the troops. He looked his usual rugged self with thick black stubble in an appearance that was most unlike most officers of the army. He paced like a lion before finally pausing to address the troops he was about to lead.

"Soldiers! The eyes of your country are upon you. Be steady, be cool, be firm in the assault. The town must be yours this night. Once masters of the wall, let your first duty be to clear the ramparts, and in doing this keep together!"

He spoke plainly and gave simple advice, and every man

appreciated it. He seemed like a god to many of them, a man who could never be killed by mere mortals.

"Stay here." Craven then went forward alone to see for himself.

Gunfire rang out as troops advanced to deal with French guns that had been placed to cover the breaches. It was the first obstacle which got the night underway, but it was merely a taste of what was to come. Off to one side Wellington still briefed Major Napier, commander of the storming division. Craven took a knee beside a lieutenant who commanded twenty-five volunteers, and it was clear he was to lead the forlorn hope, a very brave but almost certainly suicidal task. A horrendous torrent of gunfire rang out from the far side of the city as Pack's diversionary attack with his Portuguese brigade got underway.

Cannon fire suddenly cracked and shook the ground as the main breach was lit up. They looked to it and saw a dreadful sight as the French defenders opened fire as redcoats scrambled up the steep glacis towards the breach, but to no avail and with not nearly enough troops. He could have been little older than Paget, and yet he was clearly no novice to war, and in some ways that made it worse, for he had some idea of the terrors he was about to face.

"John Gurwood," declared the brave Lieutenant, wearing the uniform of the 52nd Light Infantry.

"Major Craven."

"James Craven?"

"That's right."

"Salford Rifles? Really?"

"One and the same."

Colour seemed to return to the terrified Lieutenant's face

as it lit up.

"What a lucky charm, for now I know I will make it."

Craven couldn't tell if he was being serious or merely hanging on to any hope he could find in the tense moment.

Gurwood was clearly not a man of status or privilege. He had the accent of a merchant's son, much like Craven, and that told him everything he needed to hear. An officer who led the forlorn hope and survived was rightly entitled and expected promotion, and for a man of little standing and wealth that was worth a fortune. And yet the risk was massive. Few young officers ever survived to claim the reward, but Craven dared not burden the young officer with such gloom. He must surely have known what he was in store for when he volunteered.

They watched as the Third Division finally advanced in full towards the main breach, later than expected. Wellington looked anxious. It was not all going as planned, and yet no battle ever did. He gave the nod to Napier to advance, and the orders were quickly passed on. A rocket from one of the gun batteries soared up into the sky, the signal for them to go forward.

"Good luck, Lieutenant," Craven said to Gurwood.

He took great comfort in the sentiment as he drew out his sword and got up.

"Forlorn hope, forward!"

"Now lads, for the breach!" Crauford rushed forward to lead the rest of the Light Division assault force, as Major Napier stormed onwards also. Craven peered back to Wellington who tried to remain as stoic as the reputation as he had earned, but Craven knew fear when he saw it. He had faced enough fighters in every kind of scenario to recognise it so that he might exploit it when necessary.

"Well, Major, what good are you doing here, go!" Wellington roared.

"Salford Rifles, on me!"

Paget hurried forward to lead them on, despite Hawkshaw and Ferreira being senior to him, but nobody questioned it, as they were all weary for what they were about to face. They rushed on across the open plain in darkness. The guns did not fire at their advance anymore. All attention was on the two breaches and the third assault in the East. They ran on across ruinous terrain that was mostly just churned up earth and great pits, which had either been dug out intentionally for cover, or blown open by artillery fire throughout the siege. Soon enough they got a view of the lesser breach for which the approach was an even steeper incline than the main breach. Mounds of loose and jagged rock and debris would make climbing a ladder seem an easy task. In front of the breach was a large ditch which would further hinder their progress, and the men who had been waiting with fascines to fill it had no time to do so as the advance had been so quick, they could not do their task.

As Gurwood neared the breach, shots from the enemy swept the British soldiers away with horrifying effect as canister, grape shot, round shot, and shell came pouring in and around them, and the very ground was set ablaze. Volleys were poured in on the attackers as Gurwood vanished into a smoke of flame and powder. Crauford was one of the first hit as a musket ball went through his lungs and he dropped. It was a frightful and most unfortunate loss that could have easily caused many soldiers to turn and run, but many of them had served with Black Bob for years and knew all too well he would be furious if they paused, let alone fell back simply because he was shot.

Craven took a knee fifty yards short of the breach as the riflemen of the Salfords spread out and began to lay down fire on the parapets with many other men of the Light Infantry Division, the assaulters leaping into the ditch before the walls, as fire continued to pour down upon them.

Paget took aim at one soldier on the parapet and shot him dead before he could make his next shot, but as the Lieutenant reloaded, he glanced at the breach. He witnessed a display more savage than he had ever seen or could have imagined. The assaulters called for ladders which had not arrived. Meanwhile, many tried to scramble up the sixteen-foot ditch and make the climb without them, only to be shot down to brutal effect. The superiority of numbers for the British and Portuguese troops counted for nothing here in the bottleneck where they had no cover and an almost insurmountable obstacle. Craven could not remain idle any longer as the slaughter went on. He noticed a rifleman retreating with a shot through his shoulder and cradling his rifle.

"Give that here," demanded Craven.

He gladly gave up the weapon as he struggled to keep hold of it. Craven also relieved him of his cartridge box before letting the man go on as he once again dropped to one knee. He flipped the frizzen forward to see the Baker rifle was loaded and ready to shoot. He pulled it back over the pan and came to full cock, taking aim at a Frenchman on the ramparts. He was determined to not miss, as those poor fellows below the breach were depending on him now. He took his shot and knocked the man down. He paused in amazement before going on to load the rifle. Sporadic skirmish fire echoed out all across the ground before the walls of the city with little coming back. For almost all attention was focused on stopping even a single man getting through the breach. For every soldier knew that once a breach was successful, it almost always sealed the fate of the defenders and a victory for those assaulting.

"Ladders!" a voice cried out.

They got their wish as two were run past the skirmish line. They were tossed into the ditch and placed against the scarp as explosions burst all around those trying to stop them as the bodies began to stack high.

A great cheer echoed out from the main breach, and it spurred those on there at the lesser one as they imagined some success, but also were fiercely competitive and did not want to be second into the city.

"Come on, boys!" Major Napier cried from the trench as he encouraged the troops forward, but seconds later he was shot and staggered before being caught by one of his riflemen. His arm was shattered, and he was unable to even support his weight, "Never mind me, push on, my lads. The town is ours!"

"The Major is shot!" a voice cried out.

Craven heard and shot to his feet and hesitated for only a second, realising he was about to do precisely what he said he would not. He eyed the breach and the men who struggled to take it, knowing he could not stand by any longer and cast his rifle aside. The time for skirmishing was over. He drew out his sword, and the Andrea Ferrara blade glimmered from the flames and flashes of cannon and musket fire.

"Will you let those Frenchman mock us so?" he shouted to those around him.

Paget was the first to leap to his side, slinging his long rifle over his back for fear another might take it if he left it behind.

"I am going to stand in that damned city before the sun is up! So who is with me?"

He did not wait for the response, but he heard an enthusiastic roar as they surged forward and leapt into the ditch, which was piled high with the dead and wounded. Craven went for one of the ladders where he found an officer at the base looking like a bloody wreck. It was Lieutenant Gurwood of the forlorn hope. Amazingly, he was alive and still standing, despite his hat having been long lost and blood streaming from a ghastly head wound. He looked up at the ladder with despair as he tried to find the courage and energy to make another climb. Yet as he looked up, he found himself staring into the muzzle of the French musket of a defender readying to shoot him down.

Craven ripped his double-barrelled pistol from his belt and shot the Frenchman in the chest, causing him to collapse over the breach and tumble forward into the trench. He fell amongst the British and Portuguese dead. Gurwood could hardly believe his luck, as he had thought himself a goner. He looked over to see who had saved his life, only to wonder if he was peering at a ghost when he spotted Craven.

"What are you waiting for, Lieutenant? The breach is yours, take it!"

"Yes, Sir!"

Gurwood took firm hold of the ladder and nearly sprinted up it with a new sense of vigour and determination. Craven rushed up the second ladder just in time to see Gurwood engage against a French soldier with musket and bayonet. He fought like a lion now, and he would not be denied the glory and victory he had so desperately hoped for, despite all the odds against him. Craven had seen him vanish into a deadly fireball of gunpowder and lead, and after all he had been through, he was determined to not be stopped. Another tried to attack him, but Craven ran the man through before shooting another in the leg and hacking down at his neck. It sent him tumbling over the walls and into the ditch.

Birback grabbed hold of one Frenchman and merely hoisted him up and over the wall. He tossed him over the rampart before turning back to look for another victim. Charlie and Amyn charged into several more, cleaving their way through their attackers. Matthys made no complaints this time, as he could see the horrific piles of British and Portuguese dead for his own eyes. He would not criticise any soldier for now doing what must be done.

The men of the Light infantry stormed up the ladders and poured onto the rampart under jubilant cries of celebration, which the whole army could hear, and many could see with their own eyes, including Wellington himself.

"They've done it. They've done it!" he cried as he was close to weeping.

Craven turned right and was determined to rush along the ramparts just as Black Bob Crauford had asked of them and reach the main breach to assist their fellow soldiers. Yet another officer and party of troops was already ahead of him as he went on. They had gotten halfway when an almighty thunder erupted. Craven and Paget were launched off of their feet with such tremendous power that they thought they were both dead, as the party ahead of them were blown apart and thrown from the walls.

A great detonation at the breach had sent much of the wall and many of the soldiers on both sides flying into the air. Craven landed hard and barely stayed conscious as he heard his body creak and crunch. It was hard to not think of the titanic explosion at Almeida. This was nothing as severe as that giant powder magazine obliterating the city but being so close to the blast it felt similar. A cloud of stifling dust engulfed them as Craven lay flat, wondering if his body was broken, and if he would ever stand again. Someone cried his name as several men searched for him, and soon enough the bloody Lieutenant Gurwood appeared over him.

"Still alive? Of course, what could kill you!" he joked. He carefully took Craven's hand and hauled him to his feet. He groaned in pain but remarkably stayed upright and still had all of his limbs. Yet he wondered what he was looking upon as beside the 52nd officer was a French officer.

"He will guide us in return for his life. For our boys were close to relieving him of it, Sir."

Coughs echoed out through the smoke, and he recognised the tone as Paget's. Craven moved towards him in deep concern, but the Lieutenant stumbled through the dust, holding Craven's sword, having found and retrieved it for him. His hat was gone, and his jacket was torn open. His face was black with soot and dust, and he had several cuts about his head. One of his sleeves was ripped open, and yet he seemed to wear the ruinous impression with pride. But the cloud of smoke began to settle, and the full effects of the almighty explosion could be seen.

Those leading the Third Division into the main breach had been obliterated, including most of their senior officers. It was a dreadful sight, and it rocked the attackers for a moment, but their resolve soon returned as troops poured in through the lesser breach, and those at the main one redoubled their efforts and surged forward. A scruffy and bloodied officer gave out a war cry as he ran forward. It was Timmerman. Far from demoralised by the losses, they appeared invigorated by them, as they leapt upon the enemy and would not be stopped again. Battle cries and cheers rang out as the troops poured in through both breaches.

"Come on, Sir!" Lieutenant Gurwood cried enthusiastically.

Craven coughed and spluttered. He limped on but soon walked it off, even though he knew his body was badly battered and bruised beneath his uniform. Paget, too, but the Lieutenant would not make anything of it, and they charged on after the 52nd officer as he was led by his French guide.

Defensive works built within the main breach caused little pause to the assaulting British troops who swarmed over them. They ran onwards with the few survivors of Gurwood's forlorn hope trailing on as British troops soared into the citadel.

French troops threw down their arms at the first glimpse of the filthy and bloody British and Portuguese troops who gave off a horrifying expression as though they were ready to murder everyone they found. Ahead of them was the Governor of Rodrigo, holding out his sword in surrender. Gurwood hesitated for a moment, as he wanted to take it, but Craven was the most senior officer amongst them.

"What are you waiting for? Do it, Lieutenant," Craven gave the order. He would not take the great honour from a brave man, who by all accounts should not have survived the ordeal and now deserved all the rewards one could bestow upon him. And this was the one and only thing Craven could give to him. Troops from both breaches stormed into the citadel, and amongst them was Timmerman who looked most pleased with himself.

"How did you survive that?" Craven asked, as he must have been close to the breach during the huge explosion that had rocked them all.

"I won't die in this damned country," he grimaced.

Gurwood took the Governor's sword to a rapturous applause from all of the troops watching.

"Come with me, Sir. You are safe as my prisoner," declared Gurwood.

Gurwood was gleaming with pride. It was the proudest moment of his life as he led the city's leader to Wellington with the surrendered sword in hand. Craven breathed a sigh of relief and sat down upon a step utterly exhausted and unable to stand any longer. All around they could hear screams and cries of both men and women, as the triumphant troops sacked the city as if it were a French city and not a Spanish one. Several officers ran about in an attempt to stop them, but they were powerless against the mobs of rowdy soldiers who ran riot as fires were set, and they stole everything they could find. Paget looked disgusted, but he could barely move as he was utterly exhausted, but most surprising of all was how Timmerman did not join in the debauchery and ransacking of the place.

"You do not join in?" Craven asked.

Timmerman shook his head.

"I will take what I desire from the French," he replied scathingly in a remarkable turn of restraint.

Yet over his shoulder Craven noticed a figure in a long-hooded cloak step out from a doorway and casually walk away.

"Stop!" Craven roared angrily.

The figure knew precisely who he was talking to and did as ordered, having heard rifle locks click into the firing position in case he refused.

"Turn around!" Craven already knew who he was looking upon, even though everyone else was entirely in the dark. The cloaked figure pulled down his hood and turned to face Craven.

"Bouchard," gasped Paget.

"You came to kill me, Bouchard, well here is your chance. Not in the night with tricks, but here man to man with only a sword in your hand."

Bouchard smirked at the prospect.

"If you beat me, then my men will let you go. I give you my word, because unlike you, my word is worth something," said Craven scathingly.

Bouchard threw off his cloak, revealing his officer's uniform beneath. He took out his sword with a gleeful smile.

"No tricks, for if you do, my men will shoot you dead, you hear?"

"I need no tricks to defeat you," smiled Bouchard.

"If that were true, you would have done it a long time ago. You make men scared, and scared men don't fight well, but you don't scare me, Bouchard."

They squared off against one another as a crowd formed around them. Bouchard carried a brass hilted sabre of a similar length to Craven's straight sword. He was for once dressed as per his position and not like a thief in the night now his cloak had been removed.

"Come on, Major!" Paget shouted in concern but eager to see him win.

Matthys made no complaints as it was a matter of honour,

and one of the few duels he would approve of. More than anything he was glad to see Craven finally confront his demons. Major Bouchard had plagued his mind for so long, and finally, it was a chance to be free of him. The two men circled one another, staring each other down in some attempt to intimidate the other.

Bouchard was not used to having a confident fighter stand up to him, but Craven had never been calmer. It was as if it was merely a contest with sticks and not a fight to the death against the most fearsome fighter he had ever crossed blades with. The two stopped and came to their guards. Bouchard launched the smallest of feints without following it up, as he simply tried to scare his man. It was clearly a method of intimidation he had used many times before and was accustomed to its success, but Craven did not even flinch. And that was the first signal to Bouchard that his veneer of invincibility and terror had come to an end. Craven smiled back at what he saw as a petty attempt, and now the tables truly were turned, as Bouchard realised what kind of formidable opponent Craven had become.

Craven tapped against Bouchard's blade with a sharp beat, but he then dropped his blade under and plunged a thrust home. Bouchard responded with a parry and returned a cut, but Craven had been waiting for it and had set the trap intentionally. He parried the blow, stepped in, and drove his left fist into Bouchard's jaw, causing him to stagger and nearly fall. It had been the last thing he had been expecting, and that was terrifying, for he always knew what his enemy was about to do, until now. Yet he shrugged it off as just a trick and came forward. Their blades clashed back and forth until finally, Bouchard slashed into Craven's arm with a quick but shallow blow. Craven shrugged it off and seemed to enjoy it. Again, they went back and forth. No one enjoyed the fight as much as Timmerman who clapped at every exciting moment.

Bouchard attacked with an increasingly complex series of attacks as he combined everything he knew, but he soon realised that Craven was coming back with the same sequences, as if to mock him. Bouchard tried to interrupt Craven's timing, but he beat his blade down with his left hand and seized the moment to thrust his blade home into Bouchard's left shoulder. The Frenchman cried out in pain in a rare moment of weakness.

He looked at the audience in horror as he realised what he had been reduced to. They used to be men who feared him. He plagued their dreams like a nightmare, but now they cheered and laughed as if he were a merely a spectacle to them. Yet Craven did not underestimate him, for he did not dare show off and risk making mistakes as the Frenchman would want him to. He looked about and realised he would never get out alive, no matter the outcome. His left hand reached into his pocket, and as he rose up once more, the hand came out with a handful of sand. He proceeded to toss it towards Craven's eyes, but Craven ducked under and avoided it entirely before coming to guard. A shot rang out and Bouchard was hit in the right arm, causing his sword to fall from his hands. Powder smoke arose from Paget's long rifle, which he had used to strike the French Major, and he did not try to hide it.

Bouchard looked to appeal to Craven for the underhanded play but found no sympathy.

"I warned you, Bouchard. Any tricks and my men will shoot you down."

Bouchard gave out an angry cry before running and

crashing through the crowd to flee.

"You'd better run, Bouchard! I am coming for you!"

Cheers rang out as they watched the Frenchman scoop up his cloak and flee into the chaos of soldiers and civilians. Craven finally turned back to Paget and saluted with his sword.

"Sorry, Sir, I did not mean to step in," he apologised.

"Next time shoot him here, in the heart," smiled Craven as he beat the hilt of his sword against his breast. The rest of them laughed as several patted Paget on the shoulder in respect for his work.

The scenes descended into chaos as Craven and many others sighed with relief that they could finally rest their bodies physically, and know the war was no longer doomed to fail. Few soldiers knew the significance of the capture of Rodrigo, but for those who followed Craven they knew all too well. Portuguese troops ran through the streets firing into the air in celebration and manic scenes of ecstasy. Craven rested back against a wall and dropped down to sit against it. He closed his exhausted eyes as he was dead on his feet, even as the fires raged around them, and the cries of jubilation and terror rang out, including from the thousands of troops surrounding the city. He then fell into a deep sleep.

* * *

"I'm looking for Ellis of the Salford Rifles," demanded Craven. He pushed his way through nurses and soldiers alike. He kept asking but could get no reply. Paget and Moxy repeated the same as they searched for their comrade at the hospital he had been sent to in Almeida.

"Captain Ellis?" one passer-by asked Paget.

He looked to Craven in confusion.

"Yes?" Craven pondered.

"Follow me."

They went on and down a staircase and out into a garden where Matthys and Ferrier had already found Ellis sitting amongst several invalided officers. He looked weak but alive and in good spirits.

"Captain?" Craven asked him.

"Since your promotion, I heard there was an opening," he smirked as more of their closest friends came to join them.

"Mmm, no," replied Craven in a friendly way.

"The rascal talked his way into being treated as a commissioned officer," replied Matthys.

"So I can see," replied Craven.

Some of the officers nearby looked furious, but they dared not say anything in Craven's presence.

"I hear we did it, we took the city?"

"We did."

"Then all is not lost, and it was not for nothing?"

"No, it was not. We will spill plenty more blood to win this war, but whilst our courage holds, victory will be ours," replied Craven.

"To Captain Ellis!" Paget called out in good humour.

"Captain Ellis!"

They all roared with laughter.

THE END

Printed in Great Britain
by Amazon